Hetty or Not

Hetty or Not

by

Martha Sears West

CLEAN KIND WORLD
Los Angeles

CLEAN KIND WORLD
Los Angeles

Text and Illustrations Copyright © 2015 by Martha Sears West.
Edited by Page Elizabeth West Mallett
Distributed by Ingram Book Company

Hetty or Not
Third in Series

Library of Congress Cataloging-in-Publication Data
West, Martha Sears, 1938-
Hetty or not / by Martha Sears West.
245 pages ; cm
ISBN 978-0-9908693-5-1 (pbk)
ISBN 978-0-9908698-0-6 (audio)
ISBN 978-0-9908693-1-3 (ebook)
1. Domestic fiction. I. Title.
PS3623.E449H48 2015
813'.6--dc23
2015001905

Summary: The story begins in 1960, two years after the conclusion of
Hetty Makes It Happen Suspenseful and engrossing. You'll weep with the
gentle love and chuckle at the wordplay. Picture Jane Austen laughing
as she writes Anne of Green Gables and what do you get?
The *Hetty* Series by Martha Sears West! –Publisher.

CleanKindWorldBooks.com
Toll Free 800·616·8081 · Shipping 435·753·5572 · Fax 323·953·9850
2016 Cummings · Los Angeles CA 90027 · ymaddox@CleanKindWorldBooks.com

Martha Sears West titles are available
online and in fine bookstores:
· *Jake, Dad and the Worm* · *Longer Than Forevermore* ·
· *Rhymes and Doodles from a Wind-up Toy*

· *Hetty* · *Hetty Makes It Happen* · *Hetty or Not* ·
are available in print, audio, and e-book.

Printed in the United States of America

For my parents,
Gordon and Elizabeth Sears,
who provided a home of exceptional
love and harmony.

With gratitude to my husband, Steve West,
for his fifty-five years of support and encouragement,
and to my editor,
Page Elizabeth West Mallett,
without whose wise advice and insight
I would never have attempted this book
in the first place.

Thanks to
Betsy Christensen, Steve Draper, Eileen West,
and animal behaviorist Peter Bergerson.

Special appreciation goes to
my amazing publicist and friend,
Yvonne Maddox for her selfless guidance
and so much more.

CONTENTS

ILLUSTRATIONS

CHARACTERS

Hetty Lawrence, age 20

Morgan Morganthal, age 24

Katrinka Wallace, Morgan's former fiancée, age 27

Phil Wallace, Katrinka's father, circus executive/clown, dwarf

Max Morganthal, Morgan's father, former clown partner to Phil

Mimi Morganthal, heiress, Morgan's mother

Melinda Morganthal, Morgan's sister, Hetty's friend

Leaf Locke (*Father*), Hetty's biological father

Marian Locke, Leaf Locke's wife, Hetty's friend/stepmother

Joseph Ostler, Marian's stepbrother, suitor of Katrinka Wallace

Dan and Dora Lawrence (*Mother and Papa*), Hetty's
adoptive parents

Ignatz, former employee dismissed from the Morganthal circus

Dart Duncan, an employee in Morganthal businesses

CHAPTER ONE

Hetty Waits

Hetty couldn't remember a time when she didn't love Morgan Morganthal. She was almost sick with love for him. It seemed as though dreams of him had always been there, just waiting to become a part of her living and breathing.

As her eyes opened to the beginning of a rosy sunrise, she swept back the tangles of her pale hair and felt under her pillow for his photograph. Hetty held her breath at the sight of his serious blue eyes.

She had arrived at her home late last night, following a warm sendoff from her college roommates. Now rising from her bed, she unlocked the trunk her papa, Dan, had placed next to the dresser. On the very top were her 1960 yearbook and the diploma she had just received.

Moving them aside, she pulled out a pair of well-worn elk leather boots. Dan had worn them years ago while fighting forest fires, and now they were hers. Hetty pulled them on, tucking her pajama legs into the tops of them, and hurried through the forest to the magnificent oak tree she called Hannah.

Eagerly, she climbed the familiar tangle of vines that clung to the massive trunk. With the lacy canopy of leaves above her, Hetty lay along Hannah's broadest branch. She breathed deeply to remember the fresh earthy scent of Morgan. Four years ago, she had looked down into the sadness of his face from this very place.

He had come to say goodbye.

Hetty shared the memory aloud, with Hannah. "What if I hadn't spoken to him?" she said. "He would have married Katrinka in the morning."

Hannah's leaves quivered in the soft breeze, as if to agree with her.

Suddenly the morning sky blazed with color. Hetty tried to see it as a message of optimism, but there was a dark heaviness weighing on her mind. That heaviness was the beauty queen, Katrinka Wallace. Would Morgan's former fiancée insinuate herself back into his life?

All Katrinka's ambitions had revolved around Morgan and the Morganthal business empire from the time she was nine years old. But with Hetty's unexpected proposal four years ago, her plans to become Mrs. Morganthal went up in smoke.

Hetty shivered. How did Katrinka feel about it now? Did her plans still include Morgan?

Hetty resolved to stop dwelling on her fears. She didn't want to think about Katrinka. Not today.

*With the lacy canopy of leaves above her, Hetty lay along
Hannah's broadest branch.*

The Career Woman

This was a big day. Katrinka had heard rumors that Morgan would be back in town, but that was not all. His father, Maximilian Morganthal, sent her to apply for a job at Luvliness Conglomerates, one of the many Morganthal subsidiaries.

Just inside the lobby of the spacious office building, a waiting receptionist escorted her to the open door of Dart Duncan, the man responsible for hiring. Katrinka had heard Max call Dart the day before, preparing him to receive her.

He had said, "I believe you will want to hire Katrinka Wallace." Just like that.

"Nobody would argue with the boss," thought Katrinka. "Least of all Dart Duncan." According to Tilly Teller's gossip column, Dart enjoyed the company of Max Morganthal's daughter, Melinda.

Katrinka entered his large office, and Dart's eyes widened with something beyond curiosity. When she smiled to make her dimples look especially adorable, he removed his horn rim glasses and rose slowly from his deep leather chair.

Tilting her head slightly, Katrinka flounced daintily toward him. Dart straightened his tie and came out from behind his large desk to greet her.

"Tell me, Miss Wallace," he said, "What sort of job were you hoping for here at Luvliness Conglomerates?"

Katrinka opened her glossy pink lips to reveal a row of pearly-white teeth. "Mostly I want to be in charge of some really important things," she purred. Katrinka was pleased with his look of surprise.

"Normally," he said, "I would have an applicant fill

out this form independently. However, I can probably assess the suitability of your previous experience better if we do it together." He took a moment to fill his fountain pen then looked at her. "Full Name?"

"Katrinka Wallace," she said.

Dart Duncan wrote slowly, as if to make the interview last as long as possible. His pencil hovered over the next blank. "Gender...." He said it rather to himself, then checked the box *F* for female and emphatically circled it as well. He moved on to the next question. "Married?" he asked.

"Almost," she said, blinking sweetly. "What I mean is I almost was. I would be now, except the night before our wedding, a little high school girl proposed to my fiancé. You know the kind I mean...pretending it was all about how Morgan's so kind and considerate? They're all the same, those silly, star-struck types."

She hoped Dart couldn't sense the way her heart beat faster when she pronounced Morgan's name. Was it really over with Morgan? How could he possibly choose the tall, skinny Hetty Lawrence instead! It was especially hard to understand in light of the conditions Max Morganthal had set. Max had fixed it so Morgan would receive an inheritance only by marrying Katrinka.

"He would have married me," she said. "He promised he would." She purposely neglected to mention Morgan had been six years old at the time.

Katrinka paused briefly and leaned toward him in a confidential manner. "But would you believe it? An elephant stepped on him the night before our wedding!" She sighed and her eyelashes moved languidly up and down, fanning her soft pink cheeks.

Her face brightened. "Are you?" she asked. She knew

his marital status perfectly well. He was single.

Dart's cheeks flushed. He continued as if he hadn't heard her. "What is your current employment?" he asked.

"Oh, I've never worked," she said. "Isn't this going to be the funnest thing ever?"

Dart laid his pen down on the leather-framed blotter and raised one eyebrow.

Katrinka began again. "My father and I can live on the Morganthal estate as long as we want. Daddy manages the circus for them," she said. "He's very clever, but in case something should happen to him, he wants me to have some work experience."

Dart Duncan raised his eyebrow again. "Is he ill?"

Katrinka was pleased she had aroused his sympathy and paused briefly to encourage it further. "Well, he's having some complications because of his dwarfism," she said. She became reverently thoughtful for a moment or two.

Katrinka was flooded with feelings of love and admiration for her father. Phil had advised his daughter to tell people about his condition directly, in case his appearance might cause any awkwardness in the future.

Fearing her last comment might remove her from consideration, suddenly Katrinka decided she should say something amusing. It might make her seem more employable. "If you're not a dwarf when you're born," she whispered, "you can't become one later in life!" She winked at Dart.

Instead of dealing with her sense of humor, Dart looked down at the form and continued boldly. "Do you have a preferred nickname, Miss Wallace?" he asked.

She gave him a subtle, intimate smile. "Mostly, I'm called Katrinka," she said, "but *you* may call me Trink."

She wondered if Morgan would ever call her Trink the way he had when they were little. "If only I could be near

Morgan every day," she thought. "If I get the job, I'll use the same smile on him."

She fingered the little pearl buttons on her blouse. It was easy to see why Morgan's sister Melinda would like the handsome Dart Duncan. Even though Katrinka could see he was no match for her, Dart might prove useful if she played her cards right.

He hadn't asked her age, and Katrinka was glad. Her mother had a saying: *Never trust a woman who tells you how old she is. It sounds so calculating.* On the other hand, maybe Dart would think she was just right for the job at the age of twenty-seven.

Maybe someday she would be in charge of designing those forms herself. As for the letterhead, Katrinka thought the company should be called Luvcon. A person could choke on a mouthful like Luvliness Conglomerates.

As Katrinka had expected, the longer she displayed the charms of her abundant qualifications, the more dazed became Dart's expression. Rather than further investigating her suitability for the job, Dart stood to signal the end of the interview.

"Can you start Monday?" he asked.

I Have a Plan, Daddy

The guard grinned broadly and tipped his hat when Katrinka's car approached the entrance to the Morganthal estate. She raised her chin and drove through the massive gates as if she owned the place.

In a moment she would be home at the gatehouse, behind the mansion. Katrinka knew her father would be

lying on his bed listening for her to pull into the driveway.
His old friend Max Morganthal had installed a hospital bed
in the living room of the gatehouse.

From there Phil could look out over the sculpted boxwood
gardens and the manicured lawns of the vast Morganthal estate.
Of greater importance to Phil was the bed's location near the
center of Katrinka's activities. Max knew Phil treasured every
moment he spent with his daughter.

Katrinka knew just what to expect: her father would
watch the door, awaiting her arrival. When she turned the
knob, he would pretend to be asleep. But she would hear
him breathe deeply to smell her perfume.

Quietly she would tiptoe toward him, and when he
opened his eyes she would fluff his pillow and put on her
prettiest expression. Yesterday he had said he was sure her
dimpled smile would ease his way to the grave.

Katrinka made sure the moment of her arrival was as
sweet as he expected. When Phil opened his eyes, they
laughed together as if this daily game were entirely new to
them both. She kissed his prominent forehead and helped
him sit up.

"How was the job interview?" he asked.

She squeezed his stubby fingers and cocked her head.
"I was a dumb blonde," she said, "and Dart Duncan fell
for me,"

"No, honey," he said. "No, he's Melinda's beau."

She patted his cheek. "Not necessarily," she cooed.

Katrinka thought this a good time to divert his thoughts,
so she went into the kitchen and prepared him a tall glass
of pink lemonade on ice.

When her father seemed to have forgotten her previous
comment, Katrinka gave him a crooked little smile and
said, "Do you know who gets home today, Daddy?"

"Yes, but Morgan is no longer any concern of yours,"

he said. "Even Max can see how happy Morgan and Hetty will be. You can win over anyone else you wish, but not Morgan. Why not Marian Locke's stepbrother, Joseph? The three of us got along well when we traveled together."

"I know. It was fun in Australia, and I like talking to Joseph," she said. "But there's one problem. He's not Morgan. That's all."

"Fine, honey. But Morgan's chosen Hetty, and that's who he'll marry." He folded his short arms to emphasize the finality of his words. "Not Morgan," he repeated.

Katrinka tilted her head to show she was politely questioning her father's pronouncement. "But you want him to be happy, don't you?"

"Of course I do," said Phil. "I love him like a son."

"Well...what if he loved me most? Wouldn't that be the best thing of all?"

"But he's chosen Hetty."

"Think of it this way, Daddy.... He let me keep the diamond ring."

Phil appeared puzzled until he thought of an answer. "He's just generous."

Katrinka straightened her back to appear triumphant. "Then why doesn't Hetty have a ring at all?" she said. "Besides, if Morgan thought it was completely over between us, he would've asked me to give it back."

Phil was speechless. Katrinka hoped the silence meant he was admiring her tenacity and spunk.

After a brief pause, she summarized her thoughts. "I say we're still engaged."

Phil was alarmed. "No, honey...no, no!"

Katrinka's voice grew serious. "Don't worry, Daddy," she said, "I have a plan. You'll see. I'm the one he'll want in the end."

Her voice brightened, and she kissed him on the cheek.

"He'll be coming to see you before you know it, Daddy." Katrinka knew her father was proud of his role in raising Morgan. He often spoke with satisfaction of the fine young man he had become.

Sometimes Morgan had felt unwelcome at home, especially when his parents, Max and Mimi, went through those binges of heavy drinking.

After her mother's death, Phil sent nine-year-old Katrinka away to boarding school for fear his dwarfism might cause social problems for her. If it hadn't been for Morgan's frequent visits, those would have been lonely years for Phil.

Katrinka tidied her father's covers and adjusted the pink lemonade on his tray. She thought, "When I tighten the noose, Hetty will never know what happened. But I can't tell Daddy about my plan. He wouldn't approve."

Katrinka's mind wandered to the problem of what to wear in case Morgan should come.

"I'd better have on my pink gingham dress when he's here," she thought. "Morgan can't help but notice how nicely it fits me. Gingham looks kind of homey. I'd like him to picture me with a white ruffled apron, making a cherry pie.

"But I never want to make pies. Not really. I just want to look like I could, so Morgan will get the impression I'm the happy homemaker type. Why should I have to be what he thinks I am? It sounds so dull. I want to be cherished without making pies."

The sun would soon be in Phil's eyes. Katrinka noticed it and lowered the blind a little so he could enjoy the view without discomfort.

"You're as good as you are beautiful, honey," he said.

I never want to make pies.
I just want to look like I could.

The Album

Morgan packed the car with his belongings, but his right front tire had to be replaced before he could safely drive on the highway.

After he pulled into the gas station and parked in the service lane, he picked up a carefully wrapped package that lay beside him on the front seat. It was a scrapbook belonging to Hetty's father. Leaf was letting him keep it just until the end of school, and Morgan wanted to look at it one more time before having to return it.

Morgan entered a small waiting room littered with outdated magazines and took an empty seat. Across from him a woman with her head against the wall was trying to sleep while a little girl tapped on her arm to make sure she couldn't.

"Mommy, look. Mommy, Mommy, Mommy!" said the little girl, pointing at random to pictures in a magazine. The woman flinched like a horse shaking off flies and went limp again.

"Look, Mommy! What's that?" she asked over and over. Morgan smiled at her. Her persistent demands for attention reminded him of his little sister Melinda at that age. He doubted this poor mother got much sleep.

Morgan removed the wrappings of the scrapbook and opened it on his lap. It had a white leather cover with the name *Henrietta Annette Lawrence* embossed in delicate gold letters.

The little girl came closer and leaned her chin on the arm of his chair. When Morgan opened the album, a baby picture of Hetty looked back at him from the first page. She still looked quite fragile, as her heart defect had not yet been corrected.

"Is she your little girl?" asked the child. She didn't wait for an answer. "What's her name?"

"Her name's Hetty, and she's big now," he said.

"I'm big too!" she announced proudly.

On the next page, there was a more recent photograph of Hetty. "Here's another," said Morgan. "In this one she's all grown up."

Next to the picture of Hetty, he raised a thin sheet of vellum that protected the photograph of Leaf's first wife, Anne.

Morgan thought, "It must have been hard on Leaf wondering if Hetty survived. But he knew who she was the minute he discovered her…the way her hair comes to a peak on her forehead exactly like Anne's…and the dimple in her chin."

"'Nother Hetty!" said the child.

"She looks like Hetty, doesn't she?" said Morgan.

"Why?"

"Well," he said, "because she was Hetty's mommy. Her name was Anne, but she died when Hetty was born."

"Like my turtle. Flippy went to heaven." She went to her mother's lap again. "Right, Mommy?"

"If you can let your mommy sleep," said Morgan, "I'll show you a picture of Hetty's dog."

Before he could find the page with Pinky on it, the child leaned in closer and pointed to another photograph. "What's that?" she asked.

"That's Hetty's father and her papa," said Morgan. "Leaf and Dan. They were friends a long time ago." The two men were in the forest after battling a fire. They sat together on a boulder, holding their shovels. It reminded Morgan of his summers as a smokejumper.

The little girl looked puzzled. "*I* don't gots two daddies," she said.

"Hetty has two because she was adopted."

"Dopted?"

"Yes," said Morgan. "That means some nice people let her be their little girl so they could take care of her." He turned the page. "There they are. Dan and Dora Lawrence."

"Why?" she asked, with no need for an answer. She seemed more interested in the way Morgan's eyes crinkled at the corners when he smiled at her. After giving him a bashful smile, she ran to bury her face in her mother's lap.

Morgan returned to the photographs. Dan and Dora had gathered them over the years, hoping they might see Leaf someday and give it to him.

Turning the page back to Hetty's baby picture, Morgan thought, "Leaf couldn't have cared for a sickly baby. Not after losing Anne."

Again the child tried to get her mother's attention. "What's that, Mommy?" She didn't have anything specific in mind, but slid her pudgy finger across the entire cover of a *Popular Mechanics* magazine. Morgan thought fondly of his younger sister. Melinda had been quite dependent on him while she was growing up.

Suddenly Morgan produced a shiny quarter. "Look what I found." he said. She watched as his hand flashed, tossing it high in the air behind her. At least it looked that way. Morgan reached a magic hand behind her left ear and produced the mysterious quarter. She felt in her hair, wondering if there might be more coins where that came from.

He did it again. This time, the quarter came from behind her *right* ear. She giggled and jumped up and down. "Do it again!" she said. "Do Mommy's ears!" She ran to her mother.

Morgan whispered, "Do you want to see more magic?"

She nodded. "Let's be quiet and let your mommy sleep." He glanced around and found the props he needed: two paper weights, a Coca Cola bottle, an ashtray, and his wallet.

Her eyes were big and round as she watched him juggle behind his back, high, low, and under his legs.

The car was ready sooner than promised. Carefully, Morgan wrapped the album and told his little friend he had to go.

She asked, "Why?"

"I'm going to see Hetty," he said.

"Why?"

When she waved to him through the window, he smiled and put his finger to his lips, reminding her to be very quiet so her mother could sleep.

Morgan cheerfully took the steering wheel. Maybe the drive wouldn't feel so long if he spent it imagining his homecoming. Though he was eager to see Hetty, he wondered if it would be better to speak to her parents first.

"Maybe," he thought, "when I ask for her hand, all her parents will be together. They often are."

He remembered the year a tornado destroyed the Lawrence home. Leaf invited Dan, Dora, and Hetty to live in the cottage with him. "It's their love for Hetty," he thought. "That's what keeps them especially close."

Morgan thought of Hetty's young redheaded stepmother. He shared Hetty's affection for her. Long before Marian married Leaf, Hetty was already her dearest friend.

"Marian's unpredictable," he thought, "but in a good way. She needs the steadiness of a family more than I do. I had Phil Wallace while I was growing up, but she never had that kind of love and guidance."

Melinda was on Morgan's mind again. She was the only

person in his family who really loved him and needed him. It pleased him that Melinda and Hetty would be sisters-in-law.

Seldom had Morgan felt so deeply contented as he did now. The intense expression of his serious blue eyes softened. He was going to have a place within a loving family. Hetty's parents would soon become his as well.

The Gossip Column

The day was perfect. Morgan rolled down the car window to invite the fragrant spring air into the car and aimed his contented smile at nothing in particular. From the Jeep next to him, a toothless man smiled back in recognition of his happiness.　　He sighed with contentment and let his thoughts wander.

I'm living the perfect dream, and it's all because of Hetty.

The longest four years of my life are over, and she's there waiting for me. Finally we can talk freely of our feelings. I won't worry about being distracted from my studies, now that I've finished law school.

Her parents think we could use some time without chaperones, but they don't know how it is. I feel like I'll melt or turn inside out every time I look at her. If my sleeve touches her sleeve, I can't think about anything else.

For four years we've purposely stayed at a distance. We think it's still best to avoid spending too much time alone together. I wonder if we ought to talk about how it will change with marriage.

It may be an adjustment for her.

At first Morgan was enjoying his thoughts too much to notice that his flannel shirts and a few boxes were blocking his rear window. As soon as he saw the need for organizing his unruly belongings, he pulled his car over to the curb.

When he walked around behind his car, Morgan saw a young man at the newsstand reading a newspaper. The fellow looked up at Morgan, and they nodded at one another.

Morgan stacked his shirts and shifted the boxes. He was amused to see how his roommates had labeled some of them. On one carton they had written, "Hetty is probably marrying you to get these mismatched socks." Another was labeled, "Things for Hetty to throw out." Both roommates had enjoyed meeting her at graduation.

The fellow at the newsstand looked alternately at Morgan and then at his newspaper. As he walked away, he tipped his cap and grinned. "Mr. Morganthal!" he said.

This seemed curious, so Morgan bought a copy of the same newspaper and sat in the car to open it. It was just as he feared. He'd had troubles in the past with Tilly Teller, the gossip columnist. The stories she wrote for her column, *Tilly Tells All,* could be unpleasantly inventive.

A picture of his face, taken four years ago, stared back at him from the society page. Next to it was a photograph of Katrinka Wallace posing in the wedding veil she had hoped to wear for their wedding.

Underneath were the words, *Yes, Girls. Morgan Morganthal Returns!* In large letters above the column it read, *Beauty Dumps Most Eligible Bachelor! Will Morganthal Rebound to Wed Unknown Bookworm?*

Morgan scowled. The next words he read concerned Hetty: *His young lady is not known by others in his social circle, but she is rumored to tower over the handsome Morganthal.*

There was more background information. He clenched

his fist as he continued to read the column:

> *Faithful readers will remember 1955*
> *as the year wedding plans were scuttled*
> *between Morgan Morganthal (son of*
> *Mr. and Mrs. Maximilian Morganthal)*
> *and legendary beauty queen, Katrinka*
> *Wallace. Before taking their vows, the*
> *groom was trampled by a circus elephant*
> *with the unlikely name of Blossom. Our*
> *sources say Miss Wallace has never been*
> *fond of the circus and feels relieved the*
> *unfortunate accident rescued her from*
> *that way of life.*
>
> *An exclusive interview recently*
> *revealed that the father of Miss Wallace*
> *is the well-known dwarf Phil Wallace,*
> *who now holds an executive position in*
> *the Morganthal circus operations.*
>
> *Tilly extends best wishes to the*
> *bride and groom. This time, may you*
> *keep all elephants at bay!*
>
> *Stay tuned, dear reader. In next*
> *week's column Tilly will share a*
> *delectable interview with Katrinka*
> *Wallace.*

Morgan closed the paper and decided he had better things to think about. Even now, Hetty might be choosing the apartment they would call their first home.

Nothing could spoil this day. He was going to see his Hetty.

CHAPTER TWO

Yours for Keeps

Hetty had expected to spend time looking through the "Apartments for Rent" column in the paper, but changed her plans when Leaf and Marian invited her to the cottage. She was eager to see them, so her father came for her in the car.

Hetty never saw enough of the small stone home: the sweetly scented garden enclosed by a white picket fence, the path with soft mosses between its carefully fitted stones.

At the front door they entered through the ivy that arched overhead, moving carefully lest they disturb the sparrows nesting above the light.

Inside, Marian was perched in the window seat, holding the baby. She patted little Danny on his back.

Leaf watched Hetty's face expectantly and began. "After you're married," he asked, "would you and Morgan like to live here in the cottage?"

Hetty felt ecstatic and made no attempt to hide her joy. She had never known of a home with the warmth and comfort of the cottage. "Morgan told me to choose any place I wanted," she said, "but I never dreamed we could live here! He'll love it too."

Hetty glanced at Marian, who nodded to indicate her agreement with the idea.

Leaf said, "Marian's old house needs some painting and repair work. It should be easier to do if we're living in it."

"He means my place looks ghastly. Really grubby," said Marian. "It's a good time for us to vamoose," she said.

Leaf agreed. "The three years we've spent here have been ideal for us," he said, "but it's time we moved to Marian's house so we can prepare to sell it."

As she gazed out through the rippled panes of glass at the trellis laden with climbing roses, the profusion of pink hollyhocks, Hetty thought of a possible complication. Marian's stepbrother Joseph already lived in Marian's house.

"Where will Joseph go?" she asked.

"Don't worry about my brother," said Marian. "He's appreciated our letting him stay there, but now he's looking for a place that's more posh."

Leaf smiled and said, "Since Joseph toured around Australia with Katrinka and her father, he has been hoping she might imagine a future with him, so...."

Marian interrupted him. "He means to say Joseph is totally nuts about her. You might say bonkers."

"However," said Leaf, "it may be difficult for Joseph to afford a home equal to Katrinka's taste."

Again Marian explained his words. "If Joseph doesn't really put on the dog," she said, "Katrinka will take off and break his heart. In fact, Joseph just learned today somebody by the name of Dart Duncan may take an interest in her."

"Obviously you can't know everyone who works for the Morganthals," said Marian, "but do you know Dart? He's with Luvliness Conglomerates."

Hetty nodded. "Actually, I do. He and Melinda have

been together a lot lately. Max asked Dart to interview Katrinka for a job in cosmetics, and when Melinda learned about it she seemed uneasy.

"Dart just hired her today," she went on, "and Melinda tells me he's already asked to be transferred out of cosmetic and into the circus. I don't know why, unless he thinks Katrinka's threatening to take his job."

Marian thumped the baby's back. "Or he may think they shouldn't work together," she said, "in case something more should develop between them."

Leaf reached for little Danny and took over the patting duty. "Maybe I can get his bubble to come up," he said.

Marian rolled her eyes. "Your father means he can get a good burp out of him," she said.

Danny grinned with surprise at the sound that finally came up from somewhere deep inside him, then turned to suck on his father's cheek. As Leaf did not seem to be following the conversation with the same interest as Marian, Hetty changed the course of it.

"Morgan's worried about Phil Wallace," she said. "He seems to be failing."

"I haven't seen him at the library for weeks," said Marian, "and I've missed him. I was afraid he'd kicked the bucket. He used to come regularly to do research for his elephant book. He was hoping to expose the abuse elephants suffer. Especially in circuses."

"It's true," said Hetty, "they're sometimes forced to do things they're not built for. It's hard on their bones and joints. Phil must sympathize with them because of his own pain."

"Katrinka's got a cause of her own," said Marian. "When L.C. Cosmetics tests their products, she doesn't want their experiments to hurt any of those 'cute little animals.' Oh...I didn't mean to sound so sarcastic. I should take it back," she said. "I just want her to be careful with my brother Joseph's feelings. Like she is with mice."

Leaf returned to their earlier topic. "I'm glad you and Morgan would like living here. Love is a delicate thing, and it should be allowed to bloom unwatched by others."

Marian frowned. "In other words," she said, "we'll butt out and make way for you lovebirds."

Leaf was silent. He stroked Danny's hair and carried him into the bedroom for a nap. Marian waited until he was out of sight and said, "Why do I do it?"

"What do you mean?" asked Hetty.

"Oh, you heard me. Leaf always speaks like such a gentleman. He can't even say the word *burp*. So why does it make me want to do just the opposite! I hear myself being so blunt… and using slang…Leaf would never speak like that."

Hetty knew it wasn't normally like Marian to say, "vamoose," "butt out," or "Kick the bucket," but it wouldn't help to admit to how startled she was to hear her use those words.

"Oh, Hetty! Leaf is too good to believe," said Marian. "I can't imagine what he sees in me, when I'm so awful. I just know he'll give up and leave me."

Hetty smiled. "You mean you're trying to see if he will? He's not going anywhere, you know. He's yours for keeps."

Marian sighed. "What makes you so sure?"

"For one thing," said Hetty, "he's not looking for your flaws. You just *expect* him to."

Marian stopped and stared out the window. "You're right. I do expect him to look for my faults; then I try to beat him to it by pointing them out. I guess I show him my worst side to make him stop loving me; that way I can say it all happened as I predicted. What kind of stupid satisfaction will that give me!

"The other day he said my hair looked glorious. You know what I said?" She leaned closer to Hetty. "I told him red hair was a curse, and I was sorry to have passed it on to Danny. He looked completely deflated," said Marian. "If only I could play that day over again.... I wish I could go back and thank him for the compliment."

Hetty saw the sparrows fly past the window. Every spring they began a new nest with the luxury of a fresh start. She thought of the partnership she and Morgan would soon have: a new marriage with no mistakes in it. She hoped they could keep it that way.

She smiled at Marian. "I'm sure you could make a fresh start any time you want," she said.

Leaf quietly reentered the room. Marian stood slowly and moved toward him.

"Thank you, Leaf. Nobody can get his bubbles up as well as you."

Leaf smiled cautiously. "I'm happy to serve as the...as the official burper, Marian dear," he said.

Marian's eyes were moist. "You're so good to me," she said quietly.

Hetty knew this wasn't about burping at all. Marian needed the comfort of his strong arms.

Leaf held her tight for a very long time.

The Journal Entry

Morgan decided to stop at his home first as a courtesy to his parents, whether it mattered to them or not.

He was glad he did. When he pulled into the porte cochère at the rear of the house, his father was standing at the window of the morning room. Soon after seeing

Morgan, he opened the door and came down the marble
steps toward him.

"So…you made it," said Max. He spoke as he might
when forced to acknowledge a stranger on a long elevator
ride. But Morgan hoped it was meant as a welcome.

When Morgan opened the trunk of the car to grab his
canvas duffle bag, his father leaned over and picked up the
large box next to it. This was a surprise. Normally, Max asked
Swenson or one of the other servants to carry things in.

"How should I thank him?" thought Morgan. "Too
much thanking, and he'll know it's because I'm surprised."
He settled on just being friendly for now.

"How's Mom?" he asked.

Max shrugged his shoulders as if to say nothing had
changed. Morgan didn't inquire after his sister Melinda.
They had been closely in touch since his early years of
caring for her. She would be home next week.

As they emptied the car together, Morgan thought his
father might be trying to say something, but his jaw looked
square and stern as usual.

When they unpacked some Polaroid photographs, the
one on top was of Morgan in his graduation robes. Max
picked it up and said, "Congratulations, Son. I should have
said it while we were there."

Morgan smiled broadly to show his father he appreciated
those words and anything else that might smooth past
differences.

As soon as the time was right, Morgan called Dan and
Dora. He hoped Leaf and Marian would be there too.
They were. This was even better than he planned. It saved
wondering whose home he should visit first.

They were expecting him soon, so Morgan quickly
washed his face and unpacked some fresh clothes. He

fumbled with his white shirt as if this were his first brush with buttons and laughed at his own nervousness.

Hetty's parents all gave Morgan their full approval.

Dan honked his nose and said, "It's about time you joined the family!"

Leaf said, "If you hadn't found each other on your own, I would have arranged it myself."

Marian laughed and said, "Why stop at asking for her hand? You might as well go for the entire girl while you're at it."

Dan was especially jolly. He mentioned to Morgan some details about the future when they would start practicing law together. When Dora suggested Morgan might be in a hurry to see Hetty, Dan knew how to take a hint. He laughed and said, "To be continued."

"It's going to be interesting," thought Morgan, "to have one foot in the Morganthal businesses and the other in an office with my father-in-law."

With perfect timing, Dora came from the kitchen with a batch of what she called congratulatory cookies. They were her famous oatmeal ones with raisins and chocolate chips.

While driving everyone to the cottage, Morgan was too excited to eat any of them; however, the cookies all but disappeared with the help of his passengers. Dan got the five of them singing "Daisy, Daisy, give me your answer, do. I'm half crazy, all for the love of you," only they changed the name from Daisy to Hetty.

When they arrived, Morgan opened the car door for Dora and Marian. Dora just thanked him and said something about giving him privacy. They wouldn't get out of the car just yet, in case there were cookie crumbs that needed to be picked up. The four of them put their heads down, pretending to search the floor of the car.

"Don't mind us," said Dan. "You're the one Hetty wants to see."

Hetty came out on the porch. She stood under the ivy that arched over the front door. Tiny flecks of light seemed to swirl in slow motion around her like snowflakes and gathered, forming a halo in the softness of her hair.

The warmth of the afternoon had given way to a cool evening breeze. As Morgan approached, he thought she might be cold. He wanted nothing more than to make her warm…to keep her warm for a very long time. Perhaps for the rest of their mortal lives.

Hetty's face was shining with love and joy, but it seemed to require something more. Morgan thought it needed to be covered with kisses. Maybe her lips did, too. He reasoned if a few kisses were good, certainly more would be better, and he supplied them with enthusiasm.

As he held her sweet softness, she closed her eyes.

Whether the crumbs in the car had been located and properly discarded, he did not know, nor did he care.

For some reason, during that last embrace he thought of plywood. It would be appealing to be permanently laminated to Hetty like layers of plywood.

This thought ended with laughter as he realized there was no such thing as enough of Hetty.

Morgan held Hetty away from him and looked into her eyes. He rejoiced that before long they could eliminate the distance between them.

Late that night Morgan lay in the dark with his eyes wide open. In truth, he didn't want sleep to interrupt his consciousness in any way, so he rolled out of bed and turned on the light.

Just inside his bedroom door, he opened a box and rummaged through its contents until he found a small leather-bound journal with a pen attached.

In a moment he was back in bed with the open journal against the legs of his plaid pajamas. He slipped the pen from its loop, and at the top of the page he wrote *June 6, 1960.*

On the first line he printed the words *I will always remember this night.* But there were things that could not be said in ordinary words. Morgan closed his journal and put away the pen.

Closing his eyes, he could see Hetty's countenance of pure love and joy, the tiny flecks of light increasing in brilliance as they gathered around her, swirling and lifting them together, brighter and brighter until the perfect day.

Morgan sat quietly for a very long time.

In the Shade of the Bridesmaid

The sun hovered near the horizon. Its beams of gold fanned up through the clouds, decorating the western sky. High in Hannah, Hetty shared a broad branch with Morgan. Leaning back against the massive trunk, she watched the light play on a shock of his dark hair.

"Don't you wish you could fly into the sunset," she said, "and see how it all happens?"

Morgan appeared completely contented. "I'll pass," he said. "I'd rather stay here with you. Besides, I haven't unpacked my bags from the last trip." He flashed a smile at her.

Hetty's face was radiant, and her eyes became soft and misty at the sight of him. She thrilled to know his countenance was a reflection of her own intense joy.

Morgan looked down at a patch of soft green moss on the forest floor below.   "This is where it happened," he said. "I was standing right there. When I looked up, you asked why I couldn't marry you instead. That was the first I knew of your feelings, and it almost broke my heart. You seemed so young."

"I *was* young. I still can't believe I spoke out," said Hetty, " but I was desperate." Her cheeks colored. "Maybe it was Hannah giving me the courage."

"You think so?" Morgan was quiet for a time.

He began again. "When I saw you were crying," he said, "I think I would have done anything to stop your unhappiness. After that, I couldn't go through with the wedding. You can't imagine how I wanted to stay here with you, Hetty."

Hetty sighed. "It was hard having you leave me," she said, "but I knew you had to go explain it to your father."

"And to Katrinka," he said. "I think Dad already suspected how I felt about you."

"Also," said Hetty, "he knew I had another year of high school."

"That's right. I was sure he'd think it was crazy and take his time saying so."

Hetty laughed. "And I thought you'd be right back with me!" she said.

Morgan's expression became more serious. "When I wasn't, it's a wonder you didn't think I was heartless. That's probably what bothers me most."

"Oh, I never once thought that of you," said Hetty, "but after a few hours, I wondered if I could have just imagined it, because it all seemed so unreal. It still does."

Morgan stared into the distance. "Unreal. That's the word for it. I remember seeing all the party tents behind the house and pink carpets leading to the dance floor. The caterers were hanging brass lanterns and pink ribbons all over the place."

"And the wedding gifts," said Hetty. "You told me there were presents stacked high on the gatehouse porch."

Morgan smiled at Hetty. "Complicated as it looked," he said, "I was at peace with my decision.

"I was afraid you might be too young to know your own mind. Still, it was you I wanted."

The power of Hetty's emotions stopped her breath and seemed to make the sky open wide, drawing them together high into the clouds. She could feel her heart beating with the unspoken words of her love. When should they marry?

"Now!" she thought. "Now, Morgan!" Her head was still spinning in the clouds. She closed her eyes and gripped a branch, hoping to calm her breathing and become realistic.

She heard Morgan's voice again. "When I found my father," he said, "he was in the elephant pen with Blossom. I went in to talk to him, and that's all I remember, until I was in the hospital calling your name.

"First thing tomorrow," he said, "I want to thank Leaf and Marian and make sure they're not just moving out so we can move in."

"I wondered about that too," said Hetty, "but I'm convinced they have other reasons as well."

Her thoughts went to the recent conversation between Marian and her father. She realized the pleasant atmosphere of the cottage could not guarantee happiness for everyone in it, but such had been her vague impression until recently.

When next he spoke, Morgan watched Hetty's face closely. "If I ever appeared patient these last four years, I hope you know it was just an act. Maybe there's nothing to delay our wedding now," he said. "It can happen whenever you like."

Hetty sensed he was trying to disguise the extent of his eagerness, and it pleased her that he was unsuccessful. She was relieved that the passage of time would soon end the agony of her being too young. Hetty put her hand in his.

For the moment she would limit her expression of enthusiasm. There was something she had to discuss.

"Morgan," she said, "do you think we'll always get along with each other?"

"You're wondering if we'll walk on rose petals the rest of our lives?" he said. "And I'll never snore or leave the cap off the toothpaste?"

"No, I mean really. I heard a couple shouldn't marry till they've had at least one argument."

"Why's that?" he asked.

"I guess so they'll learn how to resolve their differences."

Hetty realized this would be an entirely new idea to him. Over the years, Morgan had learned quite enough about arguments from his father. They usually ended with his father striking him, although recently a friendship was developing between them.

"Does that make sense?" he asked. "If you really feel that way, we could have an argument right now and get it over with."

"Oh...what should we argue about?" she asked.

He offered an idea: "We could argue about what to argue about."

Hetty saw the foolishness of her suggestion, but Morgan insisted on taking her seriously. He lowered his eyebrows to set the stage. But he suggested that if he put one arm around her waist, it might not interfere with a successful argument.

"A lot of people disagree about finances," he said, trying

to sound gloomy. "It seems like one or the other wants to spend so much that there's no money left for necessities. But I hope to make enough. And I doubt our needs will be extravagant."

Morgan took her hand. "I would still love to get you a ring so people will know you belong to me. I sympathize with your idea of a small wedding, but you don't need to be frugal."

"It's not that," said Hetty. "I just don't want to have anything big and complicated. Nothing to outweigh the importance of the vows we make," she said. He nodded in agreement.

"Have you decided on bridesmaids?"

"Oh, yes," she said. "Melinda and Marian."

"You might consider another bridesmaid," he said. "I'm thinking of the one who got us together."

Hetty did not want Katrinka for a bridesmaid. It would never do! It was not like Morgan to suggest such a thing. True, Katrinka had finally confessed that she heard Morgan call out the name "Hetty," when he was delirious in the hospital. It had made all the difference.

But a bridesmaid? Oh, dear…maybe they would have an argument after all. How could she explain to him her objections?

She didn't need to. Morgan patted a large bough affectionately and looked up through the graceful canopy of leaves. "Here's your bridesmaid," he laughed.

"Hannah."

The Plan

On the other side of town, Ignatz looked out his greasy window to the Alley below. Katrinka Wallace had come like she said she would. Man, talk about classy!

He glanced nervously around the darkened room behind him. All three chairs were piled high with his Captain Marvel comic books. Luckily, he had thought to arrange his bodybuilding magazines on the chair nearest the door. That way she could see he believed in self-improvement.

Ignatz meant to brush his teeth yesterday, but he got so busy, what with washing the grease out of his Sunday tee shirt and trying to find a piece of rope to hang it from. Maybe she could still understand him if he spoke with his lips covering his upper teeth.

Actually it was lucky his best shirt hadn't gotten dry in time. If it had, he would have worn it. The hairs on his chest showed better in this one.

Katrinka stood in the alley and looked up. Had she come to the right place? Just to be sure, once more she checked the directions Ignatz had given her. Her eyes studied a door in the wall three stories up, and she stiffened her spine. Anything to win Morgan.

Katrinka hoped to make it to the top without touching the rusty railing. Feeling in her purse, she removed the satin cover from her powder compact and held it to keep from soiling her white gloves.

Carefully she wound her way up the fire escape outside the building, stepping on tiptoe to avoid catching her dainty high heels in the grating. At the second landing, she ducked under a clothesline to avoid brushing her hair against the dingy tee shirt hanging from it.

She reached the top landing in a cloud of perfume, and Ignatz met her at his open door. She was relieved that she wouldn't have to touch the doorknob.

"Oh, Ignatz, you're such a darling. It's so dear of you to see me!"

To demonstrate he was the sort of gent to treat a lady with respect, Ignatz spit on his hands and smoothed back his hair.

"I know there's guys with metter banners than me," he said. "I mean better…you know. Anyways, I'm real honored to have you distinctify my abode and all," he said. "To be entirely fictitious, I thought you was coming later, your ladyship ma'am."

"Oh, Ignatz, it's just that I could hardly wait to see you!" Her little white teeth gleamed.

He covered his upper teeth with his lip. "Mmm!" he replied.

"Now that you've left the circus," she crooned, "the animal shows just aren't the same. It's such a dreadful loss!" She appeared likely to faint from the deep sorrow she suffered over his dismissal.

Ignatz flexed the muscles of his left arm; the one with the dancing girl tattoo. He made her move like she was doing the hula. "Well, ma'am….thanks, ma'am." It appeared difficult for him to think up the right words while flexing his bicep.

She pouted prettily. "And it's so unfair!" she said.

He puffed out his chest.

Katrinka knew when she was having the desired effect. She winked at him. "I'm here because…well, it seems only right that we should play a little trick on Morgan, don't you think?" she said sweetly.

"You mean like a April Fool's joke?" he said. "Naw! Ignatz shook his head. "I got me enough troubles. I mean he's my boss, kinda like."

"You mean was. But who's in the right, dear Ignatz?" She batted her long eyelashes, recently purchased from the Fanatalash Trulash Company, and displayed the dimples she could boast were her very own. "You were only doing what was necessary to control the horses," she said.

"Yeah, that's me. Doing my best…. Always doing my best, ma'am."

"Oh, I can see that. Why didn't Morgan see it that way?" She cocked her head sympathetically and sighed like a real princess might do. "I just know you can help me, Ignatz."

Ignatz said, "I ain't no Prince Charming, but if you need help…." He turned his hula dancer directly toward Katrinka and caused it to dance.

Katrinka noticed it for the first time. Her eyes popped open. Perhaps it was some sort of a cultural gesture meant to honor a lady.

"You sure your husband won't be mad?" asked Ignatz.

Katrinka blinked at the word, *husband*, but she thought, "Oh well, it can't hurt if he thinks I married Morgan."

She tossed her hair. "Well, I can't say for sure," she whispered sweetly, "but I can promise you'll be my hero."

"You think?" he said.

She put her hands just below her tiny waist and turned to go, swirling her skirt gracefully. "I'll be in touch," she whispered.

The memory of her lingered in a cloud of perfume.

Her plan was sure to work.

CHAPTER THREE

Talking Things Over

Morgan drove quietly for a time. He looked over at Hetty, but the traffic required his attention. "That's the trouble with driving," he said.

She laughed, and he glanced at her again. "Will you come with me tonight when I see Phil?"

"I wish I could," she said, "but Father and Marian are going out. They need me to stay with the baby."

"Hmm...Katrinka will probably be there," he said, "and I was hoping not to go alone."

"I'm sorry," said Hetty, "but Danny's sick. Otherwise I could bring him with me."

"I understand," he said. "Maybe I'll wait till a time you can come."

Hetty knew Phil was failing, and felt it was important to speak of it. "Max thinks Phil's been staying alive just to see you," she said.

Morgan was alarmed. "Dad said that? Then maybe I'd better go."

"Marian went to see him last week," said Hetty. "She mentioned how kind and attentive Katrinka is with him." Hetty watched Morgan's knuckles as his hands gripped the steering wheel. Was he worried about Phil? Maybe it was because of Katrinka.

Whatever Morgan's thoughts, Hetty was disappointed. She had pictured tending the baby with Morgan and imagining they were parents.

If only they could be there together so her hands and his would touch under Danny's blanket. Or so she could feel Morgan's strength supporting the child, and they could dream together with their fingers entwined.

Someday they would sit on a loveseat cradling a child they had made together. Maybe a toddler who would give them both tiny wet kisses. They could joke a little about its being their "project," or about how many children at a time Morgan could bounce on his knee.

Hetty knew Morgan could read her feelings. At the stoplight he gripped her hand, and she gazed at him in watery adoration until the car behind them honked to signal the light had changed.

Again they drove in silence for a time, until Hetty returned to their earlier discussion. "I know Phil has always been like a father to you," she said, "but it doesn't seem to bother your dad any more. I think he's mending all his relationships, don't you? Phil notices it, too."

This opened a topic Hetty thought they should discuss; something they had been saving for the right time.

"We probably both have it in the back of our minds," she said. "I'm talking about the arrangement with your dad. How he would have left you everything if you'd married Katrinka."

"Yes," he said, "we may always be aware of it to some degree. I'm sure I've told you this before, but Phil was in no way responsible for the idea.

"I hope you still forgive me," he said, "and understand my point of view. Since that was the deal Dad made with me, I told him I would honor it by accepting nothing from him. That is, I would plan on no inheritance if I married you.

"I really couldn't see any other fair way," he said. "Without that complication, it means my father and I can be friends."

"It was the right thing to do," said Hetty. "I'll never be sorry. I just hope you won't be."

"I know you mean it," he said. "Thank you."

Almost a Promise

Hetty knocked on the door of the gatehouse at the hour Phil had requested. At the same moment, she saw Katrinka drive away, apparently in an effort to avoid her.

Phil called from his bed through the open window, inviting her to enter. Hetty lifted the latch at the sound of his voice, and the door creaked inward.

"It's good of you to come," said Phil as he took her hand. His face looked so pale and sallow that the energy behind his greeting surprised her. Though his fingers were short and stubby, his clasp was strong. Under his prominent forehead, Phil's eyes appeared to have sunk, yet they still conveyed his kindly intelligence.

"Please have a seat, Hetty." He indicated a pink floral upholstered chair next to his bed. Hetty could still smell the strong perfume Katrinka had worn while sitting in it.

Phil looked out the window. "Morgan knows I'm approaching you about this.... It's something I couldn't ask of him. It's about my girl," he said. "My Katrinka. Morgan

says you can see the good in everyone. You'll see Katrinka
for the fine girl she is.... I know she has some blind spots."

To indicate she was listening, Hetty said, "Of course,
we all do."

"She needs a friend," he said. "Always it's been boys.
Never a real friendship. "There's Joseph Ostler, Marian's
stepbrother. He's been considerate. I like the way he listens
to her, but she doesn't seem to take much notice of him."

Phil smiled as if remembering Joseph had courted
Hetty in the past.

"My Katrinka hasn't had the solid upbringing you had.
But she's good inside."

Hetty took a slow breath and said, "It's up to her... how
she feels about me."

Phil gripped the bedrails and rolled toward her. "I
realize our financial situation doesn't work in your favor,"
he said. "Morgan and I talked about it. He thinks you're
amazing. One of a kind, Hetty."

His hands adjusted the bed tray and he smoothed the
bedding. "Katrinka's mother made this quilt." He smiled.
"It's all we have of her, so I take good care of it for Katrinka."

He began again. "Max will be a devoted father-in-law
to you," he said. "He's been good to me all my life. When
we were boys, sometimes I got treated like a freak, but he
always stuck up for me. And he claims I was the only person
who was nice to him. He was shy. Everyone thought he was
acting stuffy or felt superior, so they left him alone. It was
just the way he looked, I think. It was a problem for him,
being so handsome. Even now, I'm not sure his wife sees
beyond his looks."

Hetty pulled her seat closer to him and said, "You've
been one of the most important people in his life. Max has
made that clear."

"Morgan might have been my son-in-law," he said. "I

could have made it happen, but I saw how right you were for him."

"Thank you for that, " said Hetty, "and for helping Morgan be the way he is."

"Max had more influence than you may think," said Phil. "You and Morgan should both know that. Take his honesty and integrity...children see more than we suspect. Whatever a father is, they notice."

Phil's breathing became more rapid. "I wanted to go to Morgan's graduation," he said. His voice broke slightly, and he turned his face the other way for a moment.

"It's just as well I couldn't," he said. "It's Max's turn to be his father.

"Max is getting over his drinking problem," he continued. "I feel sure of it. But for now, I can't ask any more of him. He's generous, but that's not all Katrinka needs. She needs love and reassurance.

"I'm afraid she thinks success depends on her looks. Maybe Katrinka seems artificial, but she's real inside. She's my angel," he said, "She needs me, but she won't have me for long."

Phil's eyes searched Hetty's face. "Morgan can't be responsible for her now," he said, "so I'm turning to you. Please love my Katrinka."

Hetty smiled at Phil, hoping to give him some feeling of reassurance.

There was anxiety in his eyes. He spoke again. "I'm not asking you to take care of her for me," he said.

Hetty thought of a scene in the last comedy she had seen at the movie theater.

"Hey, Three Fingers," it went, "did you take care of Fat Face for me?"

Three Fingers said, "Yeah, Boss. I took care of him real

good. I sent him bye-bye, if you know what I mean.... He's real happy down there with the fishes."

Hetty heard the workmen talking outside in the topiary garden. She used it as an excuse to look out the window and think.

Phil isn't asking me to promise anything. Still, I know what he's hoping for.

What would Morgan want me to do? When Katrinka makes up stories about him for the gossip column, he simply turns the other cheek...says she's probably trying to build her self-confidence.

There's nothing to be lost by trying to have good feelings about her. I suppose I need to love Katrinka, but if I place conditions on it, is it really love?

Phil's not making demands. That means if I do as he wishes, I'll be having those feelings of my own free will.

A promise—almost any promise—is too big for me. Unless I really think it through first. I have to know it won't be an impossible commitment.

How can anything about love be a bad promise?

I must think how it would feel to be Katrinka.... To be the one who lost Morgan.

Phil's eyes closed. "Thank you for listening to an old man rant," he said. The energy was gone from his voice.

"I don't think of it that way at all," said Hetty. "It's a privilege to be with you."

Poor Thing

Morgan planned to study for the bar exam most of the morning, but before spreading out his books he wanted to spend some time with Phil.

There was a story he had heard in his law school about John Foster Dulles. It was rumored Dulles had learned how many correct answers were necessary in order to pass the bar exam. Two-thirds were required, so after answering just two-thirds of the questions he closed his exam and handed it in.

The fact that Dulles had passed was irritating to Morgan's classmates. But Morgan thought the story would be interesting to Phil. Phil Wallace often advised against flirting with chance, or living life on the brink in such a way.

As Morgan strolled across the lawn to see Phil at the gatehouse, he saw his father's Rolls Royce had been pulled out from the carriage house. The chauffeur had brought it out of hiding and was polishing it in the side driveway.

Morgan understood the man's motivation. Katrinka was nearby admiring his work. Upon seeing Morgan, she came out from behind the car, tossed her hair in the sun and smiled.

"Do you remember when we were children," she said, "and Daddy used to drive us to the beach?"

"Of course."

"You were my sweet hero, even then." Katrinka tilted her head and laughed her life-on-the-brink laugh. She leaned back against the fender, and her hand caressed the sleek panel of the door, as if to show how good she was at caressing things.

"No matter how Daddy tried to brush off our feet," she

said, "we always managed to get the seats sandy anyway."

Katrinka's eyes assumed a wistful expression. "Didn't we have fun being children together?"

Morgan nodded.

She lowered her head to prepare him for the tragedy of what she was about to utter. "It's such a shame Hetty can't have children," she said.

"What do you mean by that?" He hoped she couldn't sense how her words had startled him.

"Well," she said, "of course the poor thing *could* have children if she wanted to take the chance on, you know... *living*." She added the final word in a whisper, as if wishing to soften its impact.

"I'm talking about her bad heart," she added.

Morgan looked at Katrinka quizzically, in case she planned any further explanation. Her expression became even more sympathetic.

"You would have been such a darling daddy," she said.

Though her smile was suitably restrained, her dimples were generously employed to cheer him.

It seemed to Morgan as if Katrinka deliberately posed so that he might see the marvelous health of her body, which he did. And her heart, which beat with robust regularity and fervor, did not go entirely unnoticed.

Morgan's face was without expression. Silently, he looked toward the gatehouse to make it known he would be on his way to see Phil.

A Box of Candied Fruit

The warm morning breeze carried the sweet, earthy scent of boxwood. Hetty breathed deeply and sat on a cool rock that served as the front step to the cottage.

The violets at her feet, though usually low, were becoming unruly, and would soon give serious competition to the lavender phlox. The bushes and vines were now spreading with charming abandon, yet the garden appeared well loved in spite of Leaf's recent absence.

Hetty closed her eyes and listened for Morgan. Often it seemed his thoughts and actions were known to her through nothing more than her wanting it so.

Morgan came and stood quietly a short distance away, absorbed in watching her. Hetty's lips were the delicate pink of the climbing roses on the trellis, and her hair spilled lightly over her shoulders in undisciplined puffs.

Much as Hannah had been to Hetty, so also was the cottage. She kept parts of her world private as she had in her earlier years. Morgan honored that, and was hesitant to approach a place that was sacred to her. He would wait for her eyes to open and invite him near.

Hetty felt his presence before hearing him. Her delight at the sight of Morgan was the clear statement of trust he had come to expect, and finding nothing guarded in her gaze, he was soon by her side.

There was an aura of kindness about the cottage and its surroundings. It seemed not so much to invite intimacy or familiarity as to promise the unfolding of gentle thoughts and forgiveness. The garden seemed to foretell the burgeoning of kindly love guarded by reverence.

With quiet contentment, together they watched a ladybug cross the velvet moss between steppingstones, until an idea formed in Hetty's mind.

"I've been wondering," she said, "if we should think about our goals. With an overall purpose. And maybe make some plans."

She was thinking about sharing ideas for a useful and happy life together, and especially about what kind of family they hoped to raise.

Morgan looked around the garden. "Maybe we don't really need a plan," he said. "We could almost wait till after we lose complete control, though I suppose it'd be more work. Maybe when it gets too bad I'll feel differently. It's the kind of thing that could happen while we're busy setting up housekeeping."

Hetty's quizzical look required an explanation, so Morgan said, "Maybe we could make the worst things into the best?"

This pessimism about their marriage surprised Hetty; however, she didn't wish to contradict him too abruptly.

She said, "But everything's right and good, don't you think? And there's nothing I would change about you. I just thought...."

It was Morgan's turn to be puzzled.

"Yes, yes...I mean oh, I wasn't thinking of anything like that!" He threw his head back and laughed until his face was quite red. Hetty could barely make out the words, "lose," and "control."

When he could speak clearly again, he said, "Of course! That still works. We'll make good things better. That will be a good mission statement for our lives, if not the garden."

"You thought I meant the garden?" Hetty wrinkled her nose. She had her own spell of turning pink with mirth. She put her head on his shoulder as they laughed together.

"This is like an interview I read about," he said. "Back in December a few ambassadors were asked separately what they wanted for Christmas.

"The first one said he wanted lasting peace on earth, and the next wanted no child to go to bed hungry," he continued. "Another wanted something like the leaders of the world to make good trade agreements. It went on like that."

Hetty felt the presence of her dear father Leaf.

Morgan grinned. "Then the last ambassador said what he wanted was a box of candied fruit." Hetty turned to see the laughter in his eyes.

"That's not fair!" said Hetty. "The interviewer should have told the last one about what the others said. It sounds like the kind of thing Tilly Teller would do."

Morgan laughed. They breathed deeply. The pleasure of their closeness made the breezes smell especially fresh and sweet.

"About your mission statement idea," he said, "and having a purpose in mind…. My goal is quite simple. For too long, I've just seen you in my dreams. Now I want to find you're still there when I open my eyes." He slipped one arm around her waist. Hetty felt herself melting with love for him. She wanted to help him accomplish his goal at the soonest date possible.

Morgan was silent for a moment then he reached down to pick a violet from between the stepping stones. The firm set of his jaw indicated his thoughts had become suddenly distant.

After inspecting the blossom closely for a very long time, he clenched it in his fist. When he opened his hand, the flower was limp, and his hand was stained. Hetty wondered at the profound sorrow in his eyes.

"This is what my parents have done to each other," he said. There was a stiffness to his voice. "I wonder how much of my father is in me." He put his head in his hands.

Hetty touched her hand to his cheek. "Just because this one's crushed," she said, "it doesn't mean everything has to turn out that way." She picked a second violet. Opening his other hand, she placed it carefully in the palm. "We'll make everything work, Morgan. You'll see."

She thought of Marian's fear that Leaf would stop loving her, and thought, "I'll try not to be so fragile."

Hetty waited for Morgan's heaviness to lift and asked, "Did you bring a tape measure?" He produced one and they rose to lift the latch and enter the front door. They had come to take a few measurements in what would soon be their first home.

Though now vacant, the cottage reflected the essence of its former inhabitants. Hetty felt the presence of her dear father Leaf: his long agile fingers on the strings of his violin, the softness of his kind gray eyes.

Whenever he and Hetty performed together, her papa Dan was the most enthusiastic member of the audience. Hetty looked at Dan's favorite overstuffed chair and she could picture him applauding loudly, pausing only to wipe his eyes or honk his nose into a large handkerchief.

The piano seemed ready to play of its own volition. Music made earlier in this place brought many memories to life, even now. Hetty fingered the ivory keys.

Morgan walked alone past the cozy window seat in the sunroom. Fragrant sprigs of lavender from the garden were tucked into the crisp white curtains where they were tied back. This was a home that invited pleasant conversation in every one of its small rooms.

Morgan paused where Leaf and Marian had placed Danny's crib. From the next room, he could hear Hetty playing Brahms' familiar lullaby.

When Morgan was in law school, Marian and Leaf had sent him a birth announcement with a picture of their baby Danny the day he was born. They tucked in a note that said, "Notice who wrote the poem inside the announcement." Morgan now saw that same poem on the wall. It hung from a blue satin ribbon in a deep blue frame.

He froze in place before it. Hetty had penned it in careful calligraphy. From the time he received the poem, Morgan knew Hetty was longing to be a mother. His eyes were once again drawn to her words:

NEWBORN

Puffy eyes and waxy skin,
Swollen nose and shapeless chin;
Sometimes purple, sometimes pink,
I hardly know what I'm to think!

Wrinkled cheeks of apple red;
Wobbly little velvet head
Uncluttered by the mop of hair
I had been expecting there!

Limbs akimbo, like a bug
Snugly wrapped in a gingham rug.
We rejoice that such perfection
Made it through divine inspection.

—by Hetty Lawrence,
proud sister of Danny

In his journal that day Morgan had written, "I will love watching Hetty's face when she looks at our first baby. I love watching her face anyway. She's made to be a mother, and I love her."

Morgan opened his hand to see the stain of the crushed flower still there. He tried to shake off his sadness.

Hetty joined him by the framed poem. Her voice was happy. "About our purpose," she said, "when we're parents…isn't that when we'll know?"

He dropped the measuring tape as she put her hand in his.

CHAPTER FOUR

Probably Both

When Morgan left, Hetty remained on the front porch for a time. She sat very still to allow the sparrows to perch undisturbed in the ivy above her.

It gave her a chance to think.

I see so many ways marriage affects people. Or maybe it's the other way around, and it's people who affect marriage. Probably both.

After Marian and Father were married, Marian had to do a lot of adjusting in a really short time. She even told me once, "Much as I love Leaf, I didn't sign up for this!"

The telephone rang, and Hetty hurried inside to answer it. It was Marian. Was she laughing or crying? Hetty couldn't tell for sure, but she kept listening.

Marian said, "I was wiping out the ice compartment with a wet rag."

Hetty asked, "Were you defrosting it?"

"Well...I didn't get that far." Marian sniffed. "My hands were wet, and my fingers got stuck to the freezing unit. I finally got one shoe off so I could dial the phone with my toes, but Danny was screaming so loud it didn't do any good to yell at the operator."

"Are you okay now?"

Marian was unable to answer, as long as her description of the incident was still tumbling forth.

"I was frozen in place till Leaf came home. Why couldn't I at least have frostbite from exploring the North Pole or something exciting like that?" she wailed. "But getting stuck to the freezer! I feel so stupid."

"Does it hurt?"

This time Marian had a ready answer. "I thought I was going to die of the pain!" she said. "But you know the worst thing about it? It doesn't look like anything at all!"

Again Hetty heard an indistinguishable combination of laughing and crying.

"I'm coming over," she said.

When Hetty entered the house, Marian was asleep on the couch with her head in Leaf's lap. Immense white bandages covered her right hand, and a medical book lay open on the floor.

Leaf stroked his wife's hair while watching over the baby, who was precariously draped across the body of his miserable mother.

As Hetty lifted Danny and took him to the rocking chair, Leaf smiled. His gentle face glowed with contentment.

Hetty knew her father had signed up for moments exactly like this one.

The Charging Bull

Ignatz slumped down in the couch and glared at his TV. A guy can take only so much culture at one time. He knew he'd never be like Johnny Cash anyway, with his really terrific hair and all.

But Ignatz wasn't going to let that get him down. He got up and switched the knob over to the roller derby on the next channel. Soon he was cheering for the girl who looked sort of like Katrinka. At least she might have, if she'd been prettier.

His fingers felt for a potato chip between the cushions of the couch. He dug it out and held it up in front of his eye. It was a truly amazing chip. He marveled at how it could block out the entire TV screen, yet it was only the size of a fifty-cent piece. He held it close to his eye then found if he poked it carefully under his eyebrow, it would stay in place like a monocle.

He raised his chin high and thought, "I could look like one of them stuffy guys in the theater." He ate it before getting salt in his eye.

The Katrinka-looking girl grabbed the skater nearby who seemed to annoy her. "That's the way. Smack her again!" he said aloud. "You're good and scrappy. Like my Katrinka." The skaters kept right on circling. He wondered if it even mattered what the rules of the game might be. Most likely they were just supposed to look good and keep moving.

He strolled into the bathroom, where he steamed the mirror with his breath. After Ignatz used his hand to wipe it clean, the reflection looking back at him appeared even better than he had remembered.

"She wants to show that Morganthal guy what a real

man looks like," he thought. "Maybe we can parade around and he'll see how she likes me. It'll serve him right, the way he sacked me. Like she says, I was just doing my job."

He leaned closer to the mirror and flared his nostrils a few times, along with the background music. "Not bad," he thought. "Sort of like a charging bull or something. I can't keep them that way for long, but I look real tough that way."

He checked his bicep to see if it had become any larger in the last hour or so. Maybe it had a little.

"Nobody'll dare call me by my real name," he thought. "Leastwise not to my face. He tried flaring one nostril at a time. He was unsuccessful, however, and decided to experiment with his eyebrows instead.

Ignatz considered his most painful problem and scowled. "Pa swears it wasn't his fault I got christened Beverley," he thought. "Says he couldn't help it if Ma was proud of her family name."

He heaved a sigh. "Pretty soon I'll be a hero. It won't be long now," he thought. "But they better call me Ignatz."

To the Cleaners

A soft breeze rustled Hannah's leaves. Hetty looked down through the thick foliage and watched Morgan climb to the branch where she sat. She thrilled at the ease and grace with which he moved, and breathed deeply with anticipation.

The smell of his exertion was uniquely his.... Earth and sky washed clean by a spring rainfall. Eagerly she took it for her own as it reached her nostrils.

When Morgan was beside her, she struggled to keep her mind on the matter she had planned to discuss. "I think your mother wants to be happy again," she said. "I mean with your father."

Morgan lowered his dark eyebrows. "I'm not so sure. It could be she likes being unhappy. It's as if she gets some perverse satisfaction out of it. Like she's trying to prove something."

Hetty had wondered about that herself. What could Morgan's mother, Mimi, be trying to prove?

Maybe she hopes someday we'll look in her coffin and say, "Oh the poor, tragic woman! If Max had really loved her, he would have disappeared quietly so she could marry someone her parents picked out—someone who wasn't so handsome."

Or maybe we're supposed to think, "Max should have suspected Mimi was younger than she said, so it's all his fault. And did he really expect love to last between a socialite and a clown? It was cruel of him to marry her."

If Mimi thinks Max married her for her money, maybe that's why she drowned her sorrows in drink. Subconsciously, does she want us to see it that way?

Morgan looked down at the leaves on the forest floor. "My mother has too many problems," he said, "and they won't change. I suppose it's good that you're optimistic, but I wonder sometimes if you're seeing the truth. If you're being realistic."

"Still," said Hetty, "nobody accomplishes anything without hoping and dreaming about it." She set her lips firmly. "I think your mother wants to be happy like everyone else."

"You have a point," he said, "but just thinking something ought to be true doesn't mean it is," said Morgan.

"Doesn't it work the other way too?" said Hetty. "I mean just because we think something's not true, that doesn't mean it isn't."

The corners of Morgan's eyes crinkled as if a smile would soon appear.

"Besides," said Hetty, "I think if you want a miracle to work you have to help it along." She put a finger by the dimple in her chin. "I think Mimi and I can be friends. In fact I'm sure of it."

Morgan considered Hetty's words and brushed his knuckles against his jaw as a signal that he was skeptical, but attentive.

It was a small gesture, but like so many others, it made Hetty's knees feel weak with love for him. She would treasure the image of it.

With effort, she returned to the matter they had been discussing. "I love the portrait of your mother when she was married," said Hetty. "I try to imagine how she felt in her white dress, when they were just starting out together. When she sees that painting, it must bring back those same feelings...at least some of the time."

Morgan shook his head. "Just so you know," he said, "Mom and Dad had already eloped when her parents got her that wedding dress. They told my mother she didn't deserve to wear white, because of getting married without their approval. My grandparents never let her forget it. Even though they bought it for her, they made sure she felt ashamed before they forced her to wear it.

Hetty's eyes widened. "You mean they made her feel guilty and then had her wear it anyway?" she said. "That would have hurt them both."

Morgan cracked his knuckles. "According to Phil," he said, "Dad was furious and told Mom's parents they didn't want a reception. Then to defend the virtue and purity of his new bride, my father took all the blame. He claimed he was the only one responsible for their eloping.

"I'm afraid he was so convincing that my mother

believed it. She was torn between loyalty to her parents and her husband. She was young, and still under her father's thumb," said Morgan. "The next low point for them was two years later, when I was born." Morgan smiled as if to say, "Don't worry, I can live with the idea."

Hetty thought again of Mimi's portrait and the flawless features that lacked expression even then. Her face looked as blank as the white dress she wore.

"Did you know," said Hetty, "why Japanese brides wear white? It's an interesting custom. The dress is symbolic of the future with her husband. Sort of like a clean slate for him to write on."

"Well," said Morgan, "my mother doesn't seem too crazy about what Dad has written on hers."

"I wish she'd send it to the cleaners," said Hetty, "so he could start over."

"Dad would probably welcome a second chance," he said, "but I doubt if she cares any more." As he shook his head, a dark thatch of hair fell across his forehead.

"I say she still cares," said Hetty. "Maybe sometimes I want to make things be true when they're not. I may even try to imagine they are. But when that's all I'm doing, at least I know it."

Morgan stretched and wove his fingers together behind his head. He leaned back against Hannah's massive trunk. "I used to wish you were more realistic," he said, "so you wouldn't risk disappointment, but now I know better. You'd rather have your dreams dashed than ever set them aside." His white teeth flashed in a smile.

Even as he spoke, Hetty's eyes lit up with a new thought, and she blinked with excitement. Her cheeks became flushed with the effort of perfecting an idea. "I wonder," she said, "...when is their anniversary?"

"Mmm...I'm not sure. Did Melinda say it's next week?"

"No matter. We'll find out, and here's what we'll do," she said. "We'll sing to them." Hetty straightened her skirt with the air of a born organizer.

Morgan looked uneasy. His mouth formed a quizzical shape as he waited for the rest of her plan to surface. "Oh...I don't know," he said rather pitifully.

This was a man who could jump out of a plane into the path of a raging fire, who relished the adventure of soaring in his glider, who had even survived being trampled by an elephant. Yet at the mention of singing, his unbridled panic was evident.

Hetty was quick to relieve his fears. "That's okay," she said. "You won't need to sing. Father can play the violin, and anyone who wants to can join in. We'll just be an excuse for what's going to be the best part."

She looked at Morgan out of the corner of her eye. "How often does Mimi hear Max sing?" she asked.

"Never, far as I know."

"She's going to love his voice!" said Hetty. "Remember the year he sang for the party at the cottage? *Some Enchanted Evening,*' I think. I remember you and Melinda were surprised."

"You'll never get him to sing for her," said Morgan. Though he delivered the warning, he couldn't disguise his admiration.

"Maybe not, but is there anything to lose by trying? We're halfway there, now that we have a plan."

"I appreciate your optimism," he said. "Maybe it's like when I used to return my horse to the ranger station. Once the nose was inside, you knew the rear half of him would soon come. You certainly wouldn't slam the gate closed before his tail was in," he said.

"And of course I hope you're right.

"You always seem to have a dream. I can't imagine

where they all come from."

Hetty laughed and dipped her head. "I think you can," she said. Her voice was playing with him. When she raised her chin, the blue of her eyes shone with pleasure, and all because of him. He was the reason for her dreams.

Morgan's face colored, and he sought a distant view. The clouds on the horizon provided a convenient focus, allowing him to hide the warmth of his emotions.

They both turned their attention to a hippopotamus with five legs. When the cloud became unrecognizable, Hetty spoke again.

"I told your mother we both feel lucky to be alive," she said, "and there has to be a reason for our surviving."

"Sounds like you know what it is," he said.

"Well, I like to help people appreciate each other. And if somebody doesn't like me, I figure it's my job to care about them anyway. It's easy for me to love people."

"You need to know about my mother," said Morgan. "She shuts herself in her room to avoid the family for hours at a time. She lies there reading plays aloud or listening to operas on the record player. That's her life. I'm afraid you're attempting the impossible."

Hetty smiled and said, "You probably remember the Haxton school motto. *I shall find a way or make one.* The way I see it, there's always a way, even if you have to make one up.

"You may not think I could tear a whole phonebook in half," she said, "but I could if I ripped out ten pages at a time."

Morgan grinned. "Want to know a secret? I'll tell you how it's done, if you won't tell anyone.

"First you soak a strip down the center with water," he said. "All the pages. And bake it in the oven to make it brittle. Now for the hardest part: when you tear it, you have to grind your teeth and grunt, so your face turns red."

Hetty laughed. "Really? It makes the trick extra fun, knowing that," she said.

"You see? You're definitely clever enough to figure out how to do it! How to help your mother, I mean."

Morgan chuckled. "She's certainly brittle enough," he said.

Hetty sighed. "Everyone deserves to start a marriage better than they did," she said.

Spots of sunlight splashed through the branches and played among her fingers.

A joyous brilliance was everywhere, weaving them together with the glorious promise of all that was to come. It glowed through the shimmering leaves and danced in her hair.

At the sound of Hetty's soft voice, a smile came to Morgan's lips. It stayed there for so long he had to turn his head for fear he looked foolish.

There was something Hetty wanted to know. "Your grandparents...that is, Mimi's parents," she asked, "did they ever forgive Max and Mimi?"

Morgan made no answer. Hetty waited until the hippopotamus cloud had completely disappeared; then she laid her cheek against his hand. She knew his thoughts. His parents had gone all those years without the acceptance they wanted. Hetty and Morgan must make a better beginning.

Before announcing a wedding date, the two of them would need to be sure of Mimi's approval.

Truth

Early next morning they met again high in Hannah's branches. Morgan watched as Hetty reached for a bough above her. She pulled herself up, and the gentle breeze carried the freshness of her scent to him. It was the soft sweetness of honeysuckle. He breathed deeply and watched her stand tall.

Hetty shaded her eyes with the back of her hand before speaking. Her hand shook ever so slightly. "The other day, I told you it was easy for me to love people," she said, "but it isn't. At least not everybody."

She couldn't make herself look directly at Morgan. Katrinka's name would be written across her face, and Morgan would be able to read it.

"I've always thought I could tell you anything," she said, "but I lied to you." There was a little squeak to her voice.

Hetty didn't see Morgan's look of surprise, and she continued. "That's why I wanted to see you this morning. I feel like our thoughts make us who we are," she said, "and I knew you wouldn't like what you saw."

Her words flowed rapidly. "It's not about Mimi. I don't even know her yet, and I love her already. Besides, when your family's getting along well, it's exciting to see you happy. I want things to be right with your parents, and I want to feel like I'm involved. I guess it's for selfish reasons, because your approval is so important to me."

Hetty was quite breathless. "That's not what I'm mostly worried about. It's just, well…other people," she said. "I ought to be more in charge of how I feel."

She was breathing rapidly now. "I know love makes everything work better," she said. "The trouble is I have to work so hard and keep saying it to myself."

Hetty paused to catch her breath and said, "I don't like the way hate can spread and grow."

She thought of an *I Love Lucy* television show in which Lucy used too much yeast in the bread dough. The dough rose and kept increasing till it oozed out of the oven and pinned her against the kitchen sink. Hetty wondered how Lucy ever concealed the evidence.

"I'm sure love grows the same way," she said, "but you don't have to hide it. It never makes the kind of mess you have to clean up."

Morgan stretched his legs and looked up at her. His smile conveyed warmth and understanding. "When people try to hide hatred," he said, "maybe it isn't so much dishonesty as it is self-control. And I'm afraid I'm the wrong person to hear your confession. You're talking to the master of sublimation.

"Sometimes I hide my feelings for my parents," he said. "Is that dishonest? Maybe so. At times, the best I can do is put on a mask and pretend to have good feelings. Isn't that better than nothing at all?

"And you can bet I encourage Melinda to put on a brave face. I like to hope some of it will stick and become real," he said.

"Sometimes the motto I live by is, I shall find a way or fake one." Morgan watched the distant clouds. "I love your honesty," he said. "I hope my confession hasn't shocked you."

CHAPTER FIVE

Late for Dinner

Morgan drummed his fingers on the steering wheel. The line of cars waiting for the ferry was the longest Morgan had ever seen. It wound out of sight before him along the muddy riverbank.

In less than half an hour, his parents would be expecting him. Tonight was the first dinner engagement to which they had invited Hetty.

In spite of the costly and opulent furnishings—or perhaps because of them—Hetty would feel an air of cool austerity in the cavernous rooms of the Morganthal mansion.

There was no mistaking the real purpose of this formal gathering. His mother would watch Hetty in reserved silence throughout the evening. She was sure to impose an awkward discomfort on Hetty. It was clear Morgan would not arrive at the dinner until well after the appointed time, so Hetty would have to endure it alone.

Morgan recalled a conversation earlier that day. His

mother had said, "Katrinka was supposed to be my daughter-in-law. Why did this Hetty person have to come along? She's just an interloper with unruly hair."

Tonight everything would depend on his mother. Mimi Morganthal was a woman of unpredictable temperament. Merely adjusting to the changes in her own moods seemed to be more than enough for her to manage.

Maybe that's why she didn't like other people to alter their plans once things had been decided. Things like which dress to wear and who might be late for dinner, but especially who's getting married and to whom.

After being invited, Morgan and Hetty tried to think of it as the anniversary celebration of their first meeting, when she was twelve. Or perhaps the time he tried to teach her to juggle and she broke a lamp. Or nothing, or everything. It didn't much matter, as long as they could laugh a little to relieve their fears.

Secretly, they would both have rejoiced over a miraculous cancellation of this dinner. Still, it was likely his mother would welcome Hetty into the family, even if grudgingly. She might do so with unspoken disapproval, but she would be more than courteous to her.

Morgan wanted better than that for Hetty.

Dart Duncan would be there with Melinda. Morgan hoped the two of them would ease the stiffness and formality with some lively dinner conversation.

Hetty might not pass the test under Mimi's discerning eye, but his father's attitude didn't worry Morgan as much. He thought of the summer he and Max had taken the animals out of the circus to prevent their mistreatment. When the elephants and chimpanzees were moved to the Morganthal estate, Hetty worked to care for them alongside the men. Her gentle influence helped heal some of the raw feelings between father and son. Morgan thought Max had grown fond of her.

"Even so," he thought, "Dad won't appear to approve of Hetty unless Mom does. He'll watch his step around her to keep peace at home."

Morgan knew it was natural for his mother to be a gracious hostess. To make up for years of indifference, she might even try to show some interest in her children's lives. And she would probably wait until Dart Duncan and Hetty departed, before having a drink to "steady her nerves."

Morgan thought of the first time Hetty had come to the house as Melinda's guest. Of all his sister's classmates, she had been the one girl whose friendship he most encouraged Melinda to cultivate. The primary responsibility for raising Melinda had fallen to Morgan. He even went to the Haxton Academy PTA meetings in the place of his parents. At one of those meetings, he approached the headmistress and asked, "Is there some way you could help my little sister spend more time with Hetty Lawrence?"

Mrs. Fairburn's soft gray eyes studied him for some time then she nodded her head. "Hetty's unusually shy," she said. "We need to do what's good for her as well."

Morgan was ready with a plan to make it work. He said, "Maybe if they're put together alphabetically?"

Mrs. Fairburn smiled in appreciation for his involvement. "Melinda has a self-confidence very much like yours," she added, "and I like your idea."

From that time forward, Melinda was placed at the desk next to Hetty's. Morgan was pleased that his sister could associate so closely with a girl of intelligence who was raised in such a kind and loving home.

He had often tried to imagine himself seated next to Hetty where he could look at her without being noticed. He had only to close his eyes and he could see her face. Sometimes he imagined the soft puffs of her hair lifting them together into the clouds as he held firmly to her hand.

He hoped some day she would sail with him in his glider. They could rise together like birds in lazy loops, with no desire to return to earth.

Morgan thought of when he'd had a blue parakeet. In the afternoons when he would arrive home from school, the little bird always flew quickly to him, its throat murmuring soft, sweet sounds of affection. In ecstasy it would scurry through his hair, rolling around in his scalp and around his neck, so delighted it was to have its beloved boy home at last.

He had thought, "If only I could be a bird weaving in and out of Hetty's hair.... I would cover myself with the sweet smell of her. And maybe I could sense her thoughts and feelings."

Morgan breathed slowly and deeply. "I'll always want to be close to her," he thought. "Nothing but good can come of it."

Again the little bird came to his mind. It had been too fragile. Morgan wasn't sure how it had caught pneumonia. It may have been something as simple as a draft from opening the bedroom door. It became too weak to eat. Max said it was all right for Morgan to stay home from school so he could feed it with an eyedropper and keep it nestled against his neck.

That was the first Morgan knew of the tender feelings his father had for animals. It had irritated his mother, who accurately predicted it was going to die anyway.

Suddenly the loud whistle of the ferry brought Morgan back to the reality of his situation. The ferry returned empty after delivering its previous load of cars and motorcycles. The creak of the cables grew louder, and at long last the

He had only to close his eyes and he could see her face.

cars in front of him crept onto the deck in orderly rows.

A gruff-voiced man directed Morgan's car and those behind him to wait for the next crossing. But seeing Morgan, he straightened his spine and respectfully tipped the bill of his greasy cap. "Mr. Morganthal, sir," he said, "Guess I can fit in one more."

Gratefully, Morgan pulled forward to park on the pitching deck and got out of his car. He leaned against the ropes to look over the starboard side at the water, hoping to speed the journey with his vigilance.

Yesterday's rainfall had caused a murky, swollen turbulence, so the crossing promised to be slow and difficult.

Dinner that evening was likely to be equally unsettling. Whatever it took, Morgan knew he must arrive at his home as quickly as possible, for Hetty's sake.

A Slip in Time

The ferry ground against the landing and lurched to a full stop. As Morgan sat behind the wheel preparing to drive forward, the car in front of him stalled. Luckily, the bumpers of the two cars were the same height, so Morgan offered to push it.

This would not be a good time to lock bumpers with a stranger. Whatever it took, he must get to that dinner. Even if they had to drive coupled like a pair of Siamese twins.

To keep up their momentum, the two cars drove along the side of the road. That way the traffic ahead wouldn't slow them down. Finally the driver in front let out his clutch and triumphantly gunned his motor. Success! He waved toward Morgan to thank him and sped off without stopping.

Morgan felt fantastic! This was his lucky day after all;

he'd done a good deed and could still get home in time to prevent the total ruin of Hetty's and his future.

He could possibly arrive soon enough to avoid ruffling his mother's feathers too badly. He even whistled a few bars of "I've Got a Loverly Bunch of Coconuts," along with the radio, in the hope of cultivating a more relaxed and composed look in time for dinner.

Sadly, it was a little early for Morgan to revel in success. In his enthusiasm, his car swerved into trouble. Soon the axle was lodged deep in the mud at the front end, while the oil pan was hung up on a rock. Spinning his tires served only to spew mud in all directions.

Morgan had to think quickly. How do you make something like this unhappen? Some people believed there was magic in kicking the tires, but Morgan preferred a more controlled, rational approach.

Maybe the answer could be found in observing the weather. Yes, that was it! A tornado had once carried a lady to the next county, sitting in a bathtub. He would have to consider that the most reasonable method of dislodging the car until something better should come along.

Perhaps if he looked under the car, another idea could come to him. He tucked his red tie into his white shirt between the buttons and hoped he could keep his best navy blue suit clean.

Morgan found it wasn't easy to scoot under the car on his back. Nor was it as enlightening as he had hoped. He doubted Montaigne or Socrates could have done their best thinking under a car either. He was about to announce to the underside of his vehicle, "You stay here; I'm walking."

Just in time, he was startled by the appearance of two slender ankles rising out of a dainty pair of pink high heel shoes. Maybe it was someone with a car!

"Is that you, Morgan?" It was a sweet, musical voice.

"What are you doing under there?" it asked. It was Katrinka Wallace! "How can I help you, honey bun?"

"Oh! I'm glad you asked," said Morgan. "As you can see, I'm a little overdressed for fixing the car. I was about to walk home."

"Oh, you poor dear! Let me drive you. I just need to take my blouse to the cleaners before it closes. Even with that, I can get you home faster than you could walk."

His white teeth flashed in a grateful smile. "Thanks! If it's not too much trouble. I'm already late for an important dinner."

Katrinka cocked her head and pursed her lips into a little heart shape. "Well, we can't keep her waiting, can we?" She winked at Morgan as if to say, "I know who's waiting for you and why you're so anxious."

Who can say whether the next occurrence could have been prevented?

With only the tiniest whimper and a graceful twist of her slender neck, Katrinka fell headlong into Morgan's arms. One shoe had become lodged in the mud, and the other had fallen off nearby.

"Oh, I feel so foolish!" she said, languidly fanning her long eyelashes. "What if you hadn't been here to save me! You're so strong, and you make me feel safe in your arms. After all, what are all those big muscles for?" she purred. "Maybe you could carry me to my car? If you don't mind driving."

Morgan had forgotten how petite she was. It was no trouble at all.

"We won't need to go to the cleaners," she said. "We mustn't keep your little friend waiting!"

As he carried her to the passenger seat, Katrinka's lips accidentally brushed his cheek ever so gently. As a result, some of her lipstick inadvertently found itself remaining where it had been accidentally placed.

"Morgan sweetheart," she said, "there's some grease on your chin. You're an absolute mess! And don't you have anything to wipe your hands with?" She looked in her glove box. There was nothing.

"I hate getting my hands dirty," she said. "I should remember to keep something handy. Especially for kids, someday." She sighed. "Their hands are always sticky. They drool, and their noses run."

He waited to hear "Bless their little hearts," which she often added to soften her unkind words, but apparently she didn't feel like it this time.

Suddenly, Katrinka had an idea. "Morgan, honey," she said, "next time you come to a dry shoulder at the side of the road, will you stop the car?"

Soon they were on a quiet country road. He pulled over, and Katrinka got out of the car. She discreetly removed her lacy little white slip.

She insisted the sacrifice was for a good cause.

"Let me wipe the grease off your chin, sweetheart," she said softly in his ear. "Then you can use it to take care of your hands."

Morgan's cheeks colored. "You're sure?" It was generous of her, and he accepted her kindness.

As he started the car, he was unaware that Katrinka tucked her little silk slip into the pocket of his jacket.

Dinner Disaster

Hetty glanced at her father as he drove her through the massive entrance of the Morganthal estate. Though she had been here as Melinda's guest many times before, the heavy wrought-iron gate appeared more hostile and forbidding than in the past.

"They'll be lucky to have you in the family," said Leaf, "though I'll admit I'm biased."

Instinctively Hetty reached into her pocket for her handkerchief and ran her fingers over the embroidered initials, "HAL." It seemed as close to a good luck charm as anything could be, even though Hetty wasn't superstitious.

"Don't let anyone else control how you feel," said Leaf. "That part is up to you."

Though her stomach felt queasy with uncertainty, she said, "Morgan will make it work tonight."

Leaf smiled. "I'll be thinking about you," he said. "And whatever advice your Papa would give you if he were here—it goes double for me."

She looked into the kindness of his eyes and decided maybe there was such a thing as good luck after all. If so, Father would be all wrapped up in the middle of it, along with Mother and Papa. Hetty planted a grateful kiss on his cheek and left for the Morganthals' front door.

When the butler opened the door, the first thing Hetty noticed was the pair of ancient porcelain urns that the family valued highly. Melinda had told her about them. The Chinese ambassador had presented the priceless objects to Mrs. Morganthal's great grandfather after some remarkable diplomatic endeavor.

In the far end of the hallway, she saw that Dart Duncan had already arrived. Mrs. Morganthal was thanking him for a box of chocolates he had given her. She then greeted Hetty, who had arrived empty-handed.

Hetty's hands suddenly felt awkward and unsteady. And conspicuously empty. She wondered what to do with them.

I should've brought flowers from the cottage garden. I wish girls could still carry fans like in the olden days. I'd hold one in front of my face so people wouldn't know how embarrassed I am. But everything's going to be fine…soon as I see Morgan.

Mimi Morganthal looked tired. "We're so glad to have you here," she said. It was a mechanical statement, but at least she said it.

Hetty squared her shoulders and looked her hostess in the eye. "Thank you, Mrs. Morganthal," she said. "It was so nice of me to come. I mean…."

She blanched and hoped she had only imagined saying those words, but there was no comfort to be found in Mrs. Morganthal's slightly amused expression.

Hetty took a deep breath. She remembered something her papa had said: "Worry is like a rocking chair; it gives you something to do but gets you nowhere."

With a brave and deliberate smile, she told herself to think of something intelligent to say. But she could think of none of the conversations she had been rehearsing in her mind.

"Is Morgan …does…I mean has…Morgan will he, or um…arrived yet, Mrs. Morganthal?"

"Please call me Mimi."

"Mrs….Mrs. Mimi," choked Hetty.

The puzzled hostess inclined her head ever so slightly toward Hetty as if awaiting the next confusion of sounds she might produce.

For fear her question had made her sound insecure, Hetty considered saying she was merely trying to make conversation about whether Morgan had arrived, and that if he hadn't, she would not become hysterical.

Her cheeks colored, and the heat of embarrassment brought perspiration to her forehead and her upper lip.

"Oh, thank you! Thank you!" she said. But how could she address her as Mimi? Mrs. Morganthal had changed the rules. Now there was nothing at all she could comfortably call her.

She made a step toward the sound of voices in the drawing room, but stopped, realizing she had not yet been invited to join the others. Retreating backwards, Hetty caught her heel on the fringe of the oriental rug and fell noisily against a console table.

Her right arm swept outward, catching her fall. One of the matching ancient Chinese vases crashed to the floor. The other one teetered a moment as if to join the porcelain shards of its companion.

"Oh, no! I'm sorry…. I'm so sorry!" She picked up two pieces as if wishing to fit them together. "How could I!" A large silent tear rolled down her cheek.

"It's of no importance," said Mimi. "Don't be concerned."

Hetty's nose made a squeaky, whistling sound as she sniffled.

"You could use a drink," said her hostess, "to help you relax a little."

"Yes, please…thank you," said Hetty. She was thinking a little ice would be nice. Though her tongue was dry, she didn't need much water.

Mimi slipped into the little sitting room and soon returned with a glass that had no ice. Hetty reached for it gratefully, with trembling hands, and took one gulp.

Whatever it was burned its way down her throat. Her eyes widened with surprise. She coughed and sputtered, dribbling the liquid down her chin and onto the front of her dress.

Hetty looked down at the dark wet spots on her pale dress. She was relieved that she had not ruined the needlepoint on the delicate chair before her. Clenching her teeth, she contained her tears and the swelling flood of her emotions.

When her thoughts could no longer be restrained, she said, "I love him, Mrs.... Mimi! I love him so much that I can't think of anything else.

"Except how I couldn't stand it if you don't think I'm suitable."

CHAPTER SIX

Dinner Can Wait

Mimi Morganthal stood motionless for a moment, startled at Hetty's words. When she regained her composure, she indicated a small room off the entry. "The others will be all right," she said, "if we disappear for a minute. Morgan's not here yet."

She invited Hetty to sit on a plum-colored damask settee, and opened a heavily paneled door behind her. Speaking through a crack, she said, "Swenson, would you bring me a kitchen towel, please? And take care of the foyer," she said quietly.

Soon she was sitting next to Hetty. "This reminds me of when Max came courting. Everything went wrong," she said. "My parents didn't approve. They thought he'd never be anything but a tall clown. He won't even have a drink with me now," she said. Her eyes seemed blank, as if she saw nothing at all and wanted it that way.

Mimi considered pressing her fist against her pounding forehead, but preferred not to be seen in that pose. Maybe her headache would go away if she tried not to think about it.

Soon she said, "You're young, but you'll learn how it is. Keep your hopes reasonable." She gazed into the hall. "We are what we are. And when we get older, we're just more of the same." A firm sadness reshaped her lips. "Don't let yourself dream too much."

She fingered the gold gilt curves of the Louis XVI chair beside her. "Max was very handsome," she said, "and I wouldn't listen to reason. But that was long ago."

"Phil says he was absolutely the best," said Hetty, "and so does Morgan. He must have been amazing to have so much courage.... You being the boss's daughter, and all."

The topic reminded Mimi that Dart Duncan would be dining tonight with not only one man for whom he worked but two, after Morgan's arrival. She heard Dart's voice and resisted the inclination to look in his direction. Melinda seemed to be fond of him.

Mimi thanked Swenson for the towel she had requested, and she stood to blot Hetty's collar gently. The gangly girl was wearing a simple serviceable dress. It wasn't the fashionable, sophisticated sort Mimi had come to expect on visitors to their home.

As she looked curiously at the wide-eyed Hetty, a new sentiment was awakened...or was it an old one? This girl seemed to care about her. Mimi forgot she had a headache and placed her hand on Hetty's shoulder. "You were expecting water. That's what I should have given you," she said. "Doesn't Morgan drink either?"

"No," said Hetty.

"It's because of me, isn't it?"

Hetty lowered her eyes.

Mimi tilted Hetty's chin up with her cupped hand. "Is that why?"

"There are some decisions we've made together," said Hetty.

Her face was suddenly animated. "We're both supposed to be dead, you know. It's not just because Morgan was trampled by Blossom. I was born with a heart defect." She took a deep breath. "So with Morgan and me, we want to make every day worthwhile. Otherwise, what's the point? In our being alive, I mean."

Mimi looked expectantly at Hetty. An uncertain smile altered the elegant surface of her face. "Morgan has a lot of friends, doesn't he?" she said. "I hadn't known that about him. Seeing him at his graduation…he wasn't the way I'd expected."

She recalled it had seemed significant to Morgan that his family should attend his graduation. Looking back, Mimi was vaguely aware of treating Hetty as if she were invisible. Maybe she had wanted her to be Katrinka. Many awkward silences had made the experience less than ideal.

Mimi pinched her lips together. "Don't expect Morgan to be perfect," she said.

Hetty smiled. "Oh, I don't," she said, "so it always surprises me that he is anyway." Her eyes shone with excitement. "He's perfect for me," she added, blushing as if embarrassed at how open she had been.

Mimi sat next to Hetty again on the settee and studied the little pink splotches on her glowing cheeks. They faded as her blush gave way to excitement.

Hetty began again. "I think dreams are what we're mostly made of," she said, "and isn't change the best adventure of all? Morgan and I talk a lot about the things we want to do. He's going to take me up in his glider when gets it out of mothballs. He says it might even help him think while he studies for the bar exam."

"And what about you?" asked Mimi.

"He might teach me to drive."

"You haven't learned yet?"

"Not yet. I have a little problem with getting lost," said

Hetty. "But I'll need to drive if I start law school, and before the children come."

Mimi wondered what group of children Hetty expected might drop in on her, but soon realized she meant those to be delivered by the stork.

Hetty had more to say. "Morgan tells me nobody has written about his family, and I love to write. I guess it's partly because I'm adopted," she said, "but I think the next generation needs to know things like the story of your courtship.

"Besides," she added Morgan's relatives are important to me too. I could take pictures and even interview anybody who's not dead yet."

Mimi thought Hetty's idea might be a good one. Certainly her marriage to Max had a noteworthy beginning that should be recorded. And the attic contained a jumble of interesting family records that needed organizing.

Mimi felt Hetty's excitement. "You really believe dreams are what we're made of?" she asked.

She found the answer in the girl's face. Hetty's whole countenance shone with dreams that were sure to happen. Her eyes spoke of hope and something else. What was it?

There was nothing special about this girl. Or was there? She was tall and skinny, with untamed hair and wet stains on the front of her rather sensible dress.

Since her arrival, one blunder had followed another, so not even the household valuables were safe. Even so, something of wonderful sweetness had happened to Mimi. For some unknown reason, she wanted to stay near Hetty for a moment longer, hoping it might cling to her.

It couldn't last, she was sure of it.

Mimi reluctantly looked away and forced her thoughts back to the present dinner plans.

Comings and Goings

Dinner was served. Hetty looked across the table at Melinda and felt glad to be seated across from her dear friend.

Back in the sixth grade, they used to poke each other in the ribs whether or not there was anything to communicate. They always pretended to understand one another's secret signals.

Melinda glanced at her mother. When she was confident Mimi was occupied and wouldn't notice, she made a silly cross-eyed face at Hetty, pressing her nose up to make it look comical and piggish. Hetty knew why.

She wants me to relax. She's as nervous for me as I am for myself. Melinda has always been a champion face-maker. Everyone needs a future sister-in-law like that.

She's comfortable with all ten eating utensils, or however many we have. I shouldn't be counting, anyway.

Let's see…what are the fork and spoon for above the plate? Maybe dessert?

Dart looks like he'll know how to use the fingerbowl. But Mimi's the one I'd better watch.

Max keeps looking over at Mimi, too. Is he trying to read her emotions? She doesn't look like she has any.

But here's what I think: I think she's secretly trying to dream up an excuse to run to him and throw her arms around his neck and tell him of her secret longing to wrap her whole self around him. And that her desire can no longer be quenched in drink.

He'll lift her in his arms and bury his face in her neck, then enfold her in the pure white tablecloth like the beautiful young bride she once was.

She'll run her fingers through his hair and smile at her handsome groom as if to say, "Oh, my wise and brilliant hero! I don't need wine; all I need is you! Carry me away from all this!"

Then with manly ferocity he'll tip over the table, sending all the wine glasses crashing to the floor, thus punctuating this, the most memorable event of his entire mature life, with a moment of unparalleled drama.

I guess that's not going to happen with all of us sitting around the table. But I know that's what she's thinking.

Later, in a sweet private moment of treasured intimacy, they'll sit hand in hand someplace where…well, who knows where. I guess they don't actually have any intimate places around here.

Oh, I know. Max will carry her to the hammock behind the servants' quarters. Mimi will tell him how she had looked across the room and imagined him singing, Some Enchanted Evening, *and that was the magic moment when she realized he would forever be the man of her dreams.*

When her attention returned to the present, Hetty was sure Morgan would soon move quietly through the double doors of the dining hall, causing no interruption to the conversation. But she tried not to listen for him.

She became aware of his arrival when Dart and Melinda acknowledged him with their eyes.

At first she thought, "No, it's Katrinka. I know her perfume. Marian says she wears Bellodgia by Caron."

But it was Morgan, and his hand found hers with a brief but firm grip.

Why did he smell like Katrinka? She tried not to think about it.

Hetty knew she ought to listen more attentively to the conversation. Max was discussing the subject of opera music.

"The finest performance I've seen was *Vanessa*," he said.

"We went to the premiere at the Met. The best of Samuel Barber, for sure." Max looked across the table at Mimi. "Two years ago, wasn't it?"

His wife's face was expressionless, but he continued.

"They hated it in Europe," he said.

Hetty quickly swallowed the creamed potato in her mouth. "Was it just too different?" she asked.

Mimi became animated. "Maybe the critics there didn't appreciate Menotti's writing it in English. Barber worked with Menotti, you know, and it was a brilliant collaboration."

Hetty had seen *The Medium* by Menotti and had practiced singing "Old Black Swan" from that opera. The melody still haunted her when she thought of it. It was dark and eerie, but beautiful.

Max remembered something else about *Vanessa*. "Apparently they offered the leading role to the great Maria Callas," he said, "but she refused it. She was afraid the new young singer who played the part of Erika might steal the show."

With a sudden flurry of pink and an increase in the scent of Bellodgia, a visitor entered the front door without knocking. It was Katrinka. She apologized profusely, cooing at each face around the table.

"Oh, Hetty!" she said, "I just saw the flowers and fruit you gave Daddy! You're such a darling to be so thoughtful." All eyes were on Hetty as if to offer their unanimous praise for her kindness.

"No, I didn't.... I didn't bring it," said Hetty. Her face colored, and she looked down at her plate.

"You don't need to be so modest," chirped Katrinka.

"Really," said Hetty quietly, "I didn't."

Katrinka winked at Dart, and Hetty thought she knew the meaning of it.

Her wink is saying to everyone, "I know Hetty wouldn't have the decency to give anything to Daddy. Dart and I both know. It's our little secret!

"I want Morgan to become insanely jealous over my private communications with Dart.

"And I do hope he thinks I've thoroughly bewitched Joseph Ostler with my matchless beauty.

"Maybe Morgan will stand and publicly declare his devotion to me, now that he's learned how thoughtless Hetty is."

Katrinka cavorted gracefully around the dining hall to show her familiarity with the expanse of gleaming silver and all the fine porcelains on display. Then she cocked her head and looked at Morgan.

"Honey bun," she said in a whisper for all to hear, "I believe you have something of mine. I've just come for it."

She flounced her way over to Morgan, and reaching into his pocket, she quietly removed her little lacy slip. For the most part, it appeared no one was meant to see it, yet Hetty sensed Katrinka deliberately placed it within her view for an instant longer.

Her mission accomplished, Katrinka departed in a swirl of pinkness, leaving only the kiss she had blown into the air and the scent of Bellodgia by Caron lingering in the room.

Dessert

Why was Katrinka's slip in Morgan's pocket? Of course there had to be a logical explanation for it, but as Hetty was unable to invent a story in her mind, she sighed and resolved to join the conversation at the table.

The clutter of words blended together in her head with

billows of mist and Belgian lace, all flaunting the scent of Katrinka.

Hetty's mind wandered. She remembered talking with Melinda earlier that day. Melinda had laughed and said, "I'm a one man woman, and I think I've found him."

She was speaking of Dart, and Hetty kept noticing she looked radiantly happy whenever their eyes met. Hetty had advised her to just wait and see, fearing Katrinka might present complications.

Melinda caught her attention. "Is Leaf still teaching you the violin?" she asked.

"Yes," said Hetty, "but we're not as regular with it, now that he and Marian have moved back to her old house."

Max was surprised. "Why would they move?" he asked. "The cottage seemed just right. Beautiful!" It surprised Hetty to hear his enthusiasm for the tiny home.

Hetty knew she mustn't yet mention their plans to live in the cottage after the wedding. Not in front of Mimi. She caught herself just in time.

"They're trying to fix up her place to put it up for sale," she said, "but the baby makes it hard for Marian to get much done."

Soon the talk turned to other things. Mimi pressed the buzzer underfoot to request the removal of the dinner plates. The interval before the dessert course did not of itself suggest a new topic for discussion, so Hetty was pleased when Morgan filled the brief lull. His words were directed toward Dart.

"You know how Mom got her name?"

Dart glanced at Mimi. "It's not short for Miriam?"

"I was named for the Mimi in *La Bohème*," she said.

That got Hetty's attention. "Really? That's my favorite opera!" she said.

"That was a favorite of her parents, too," said Max. "After we were married, I memorized *'Che gelida manina'*— 'What a cold little hand'—from the first act. That's all the Italian I know."

Mimi looked at him curiously. It was as if he had escaped her notice at the other end of the table, until this moment. "You did?" She said it quietly, almost to herself.

Hetty decided music would be the very thing to bring the Morganthals together. The anniversary plan might work.

Swenson soon entered and presented a baked Alaska surrounded by fresh raspberries in their own sauce.

Dart's first bite inspired the pleasant humming noises appropriate for a contented guest. When he said, "Wonderful," Mimi seemed pleased that he was so discriminating.

"I told the cook not to shop at that place with the big *Quality Produce* sign," she said. "You can't trust people who are evasive like that."

"Evasive?" asked Dart.

"Yes. Obviously, everything is quality," she said, "so they ought to be more specific. Do they mean excellent quality or poor quality?" She laughed and shook her head. "Whom *can* you trust these days?" she said.

When Max appeared amused, she continued. "I went to the doctor on Tuesday," she said. "It's not to say he wasn't a real doctor. And his diploma had an impressive gold seal, but I'm never going to him again."

"Why not?" came the chorus.

"His plants were dying," she said. "Never trust a doctor who can't keep his philodendron alive." Her good humor was all the more pleasing, for being so unexpected.

Melinda joined in. "Maybe he's the best there is," she said. "Suppose it just *looks* like the other doctors can keep their plants alive. Maybe they toss them in the trash and buy replacements when they die."

Max fixed his eyes on his wife. "When Mimi goes to the doctor," he said, "I would want to inspect both his diploma and the trash cans."

Mimi's cheeks colored at his surprising gallantry. She took a sudden interest in what her raspberries might be up to, and when satisfied they were fulfilling their aesthetic responsibilities, she glanced up at her husband again.

Max was still watching her. "I'm not only interested in whether her doctor has a 24-carat gold seal on his diploma. He's got to know his stuff or he'll be hearing from me."

This conversation stopped abruptly when the door to the dining hall swung open. It was Katrinka making her second grand entrance of the evening, all perfume and apologies.

"Daddy wants to see you, Morgan," she said in her stage whisper. "I didn't have the heart to tell him you'd be missing dinner with all these charming people." She displayed her dimples sweetly.

Max and Mimi nodded their approval, and Morgan immediately stood. As he turned to leave, Hetty saw what others at the table had known all evening. Morgan wore a large smear of pink lipstick on his cheek.

His departure was as quiet as his arrival had been, but Katrinka did more than enough to compensate for it. Surrounded by elegance, she became a star born to play her part on the stage where she belonged.

Max and Mimi eagerly invited her to take Morgan's place at the table.

Hetty noticed her hand resting where Morgan had been sitting and she felt a chilling uneasiness.

How could she dare touch his chair that way! It was still warm when she sat in it. Does she feel his warmth? Maybe she imagines he's still there.

Stop it, Katrinka.... He's my Morgan, not yours!

I'd like to wring her neck and smear raspberries in her face.

What's the matter with me? Her father may be dying.

Maybe the thought of Morgan is comforting to her. But I still won't have her hands touching his chair.

Once again the spectacular raspberries were displayed. When they landed before her, Katrinka rolled her lovely big eyes then closed them slowly. She pursed her lips as if preparing to receive a kiss from one of the berries.

Hetty wondered if it was for Dart's benefit. His face was a deep red, and he tried to keep his eyes on his own dessert.

Melinda had rarely worn such a stony face.

CHAPTER SEVEN

The Lie

The Morganthal dinner was over, and Morgan returned
from his visit with Phil to drive Hetty home. Events of
the day had left him exhausted, and he knew from Hetty's
wilted look that she felt drained as well.

There were many things they needed to discuss. With
no idea where to begin, Morgan put on the appearance of
driving with exaggerated care and attention. You never can
tell when something might stray in front of the car...a fox,
a giraffe, or a water buffalo.

No. He must plan their conversation—at least the
beginnings of it. Only a long and thoughtful talk could
fully resolve the problems with which his mind wrestled.
He must concentrate.

The crunch of gravel under Morgan's tires broke the
strained silence. Their time was up. He'd need to think fast.

*I'm sure Katrinka's right about Hetty's heart condition. It
would be dangerous for her to have children. It never occurred to*

me, but Katrinka's older, and I guess women know these things.

I won't take a chance with Hetty's life. If I wait till after we've talked about the risks, she'll know I'm just pretending for her sake. I must convince her right away that I don't want a family.

I always thought we should be honest with each other, but I can't speak truthfully about wanting children. Not now. What choice do I have? I need to think how to say it.

In just a minute we'll be at her door. Should I just come right out and tell her?

Morgan was still forming a statement in his mind. The car stopped, and he fumbled for Hetty's hand.

"I've been thinking. I'm really not sure I need.... That is, I don't want a family." Morgan felt the sickness of a lump in his throat. He withdrew his hand from hers and looked away so Hetty couldn't see the lie.

"That's what I've decided," he said. "We shouldn't bring children into the world just to be unhappy." His words felt blasphemous. The falsehood made his jaw tighten. He clenched his teeth to prevent having the spasms betray him.

Morgan's mind raced with his unspoken words. He thought, "I only said it for you, Hetty! It's because I can't let anything happen to you." His nails dug into the steering wheel.

Hetty remained silent for a time and seemed to be staring at the insects in the headlights. Perhaps her mind was groping for some diversion that might erase what she had heard.

They said goodnight, and she was gone.

Morgan returned to his home and dragged himself to the back entry. The servants were still clattering dishes and working in the butler's pantry. He slowly climbed the back stairs and saw his father upstairs in the sitting room.

Max was in a maroon satin lounging jacket, reading a book and nibbling on a leftover Parker House roll. He saw the grim face on his son and closed his book. "What's up?" he asked.

The question surprised Morgan. His father was taking an interest in him, and Morgan thought it best to reply. "I told Hetty I don't want children."

"Because you don't?"

Morgan's mournful expression provided the answer.

"You're a dolt, Morgan."

There was a long, stupid pause.

"Feel free to be direct," said Morgan.

Max frowned and put his leftover roll down on the book, as if to hide its title. Morgan could make it out anyway. It said *How to Win Friends and Influence People*, by Dale Carnegie.

"I don't want her to die," said Morgan. He looked for crumbs on the floor, but there were none.

"So you lied to her," said Max. Morgan knew if he were facing Hetty's father, Dan would be giving kind and thoughtful advice, but there would be crumbs all over the carpet.

Max cleared his throat. "So, how do you suppose the Lawrences got Hetty?"

Morgan's mouth fell open. "Right! What was I thinking?"

He couldn't run downstairs fast enough. Hetty mustn't have the wrong impression for even one more minute! He would have to throw pebbles at her window to wake her up.

For the first time, he realized he reeked of Katrinka's perfume. But he'd have to deal with it later; he was in a hurry now.

Morgan heard the crunch of gravel as he pulled his car up the hill and into the Lawrences' driveway. He hoped it wouldn't awaken Hetty's parents. Dan and Dora might learn what an idiot he was for not thinking of adoption.

In the headlights, he could make out a figure standing below the porch light on the steps. It was Hetty, and she seemed to be expecting him.

Morgan hurried to her. "I'm a dolt," he said. He could think of no other words.

Hetty understood and smiled. "No you're not," she said, "and you're not a very good liar, either."

Her hair billowed over her shoulders like pale clouds dotted with stars, and he felt himself dissolving in the presence of her softness.

The gentle words, "I love you," reached him from the sweetness of her lips.   Morgan felt delirious at the sight of her small secret smile.

Moments later, when Hetty entered the house, her papa greeted her cheerfully from the kitchen. He was wearing his familiar striped pajamas with the missing button and had one hand in the cookie jar. As she sat with him at the kitchen table, Dan broke his large oatmeal cookie in half to share with her.

"You smell like Katrinka," he said. "Are you all right?"

She gathered the crumbs with her napkin and laughed. "Better than all right, Papa."

Save It

As he drove home, Morgan wondered how to thank his father. Even though words between them had never come easily, he would find a way to show his gratitude.

Flashing a broad smile, Morgan thought, "He knocked some sense into me." Suddenly he spoke aloud. "Thank you, Dad!" He threw his head back and laughed. "Now what could be so hard about that?"

His headlights illuminated the front gate, and Morgan gave a lighthearted salute to the guard who opened it to admit him. There appeared to be some bustling activity over at the gatehouse. He would investigate later, but for the moment it seemed best to get home.

When he opened the door, he could see his father sitting in the shadows below the hall tapestry by the drawing room, as if waiting for him to arrive.

Max looked limp and worn. He spoke slowly. "You're not, you know...what I said. I just didn't want you to mess things up with Hetty." His voice was hoarse and unnatural.

A general happiness still controlled the sound of Morgan's voice. "You were right, Dad," he said. "Really." He moved closer. "Tonight during dinner, when I saw Phil, he said family is more important than anything. He talked about you, Dad...had lots of great things to say."

Max waved his hand as if to dismiss all such thoughts.

He said, "Save it. I can't take it now." He turned his head away and looked toward the gatehouse for a time.

"Phil's dead."

Revisiting Hannah

The air in the forest was still, and thick with fog. Every sound seemed dull and close. High in the branches of Hannah, Hetty realized how much she needed the comfort of the magnificent tree.

She had gone many days without hearing from Morgan. He was now occupied with honoring the last request of his dear friend Phil Wallace. Before Phil died, he had asked Morgan to help Katrinka with the necessary funeral arrangements.

Phil's tastes were simple and traditional. Other than a slight preference for an ordinary pine casket, he had voiced no specific desires. However, Katrinka had strong feelings about the funeral ceremony her father deserved.

It was not the sort of event any mortuary was equipped to coordinate. Therefore it was necessary for Morgan and Katrinka to be together planning and working on it for the entire week. Sometimes long into the evening.

Hetty resolved to concentrate on what could make her feel like a whole person with or without Morgan. She inched away from a damp section of the branch and adjusted her skirt, hoping she could think better that way.

It might be a while before we have a family, so maybe I'll go to law school till then. Melinda says she'll teach me to drive so I can get around better.

Before long my life will be full of him. It's so much easier now that I'm sure of it. Morgan likes the symbolism of the white dress a Japanese bride wears —the way it represents a blank slate for her husband to write on.

He says I've already done a good job of writing on my dress myself, and I haven't left much space for him. I know he meant it as a compliment, but what I want is for him to fill in my whole dress and keep doing it forever.

I feel like I'm only half a person when we're not together. Maybe that's not so good. I should try to be a more complete person on my own, I suppose.

But it took such long years to get here...to this sweet feeling of confidence we have. My relationship with him is comfortable now.

Hetty blinked and looked up through Hannah's branches at the slowly drifting layers of dampness trapped in the tangle of foliage. An occasional drop of water formed and fell with a dull splat from one leaf overhead to another below.

The tears gathered in Hetty's eyes, but she wasn't sure why. Her thoughts of Morgan continued.

Morgan's eyes are deep blue, with little flecks of brown. They kind of take you by surprise so you want to sit up straight and smile—to be as brave and kind and courteous as he is. You want to deserve his friendship and his praise.

For years, I stored up every hint of attention he gave me and memorized the circumstances. The least of his comments were significant to me. You can't imagine the joy I felt at any sign of his interest.

When he smiled at me, my mind always exaggerated the importance of it.

I made up conversations to have with him, even when I knew there would be no use for them. And when people were all around us, I used to imagine everything he said was meant just for me.

When he told about soaring in his glider, I could picture the two of us flying up through the clouds with our hands locked together all the way to heaven.

My insecurity used to heighten the pleasure of every surprise kindness. Now the fear and suspense are gone, and love is quiet, sure, and steady. It's far better than the excitement of uncertainty.

I'm glad to know he loves me and everything is fine between us. That's why I'm not worried about his being with Katrinka.

I wonder what they're doing now. I know sometimes things can appear to be fine even when there's something wrong.

I realize if you put two people together for any length of time, they might see each other in a new and better light. That's

what my uncle meant when he used to say, "Put them close and
let propinquity propink."

Oh, Hannah…it's so good to know you're always here for
me. You're just as you seem, like Morgan. You're fine and strong,
and I can depend on you.

After one last look up through the murky air, Hetty
sighed deeply. She turned slowly to leave and then
descended from Hannah.

On her way to the ground, she gripped the thick vines
clinging to the trunk. The tangled network was familiar
to her hands, yet she slipped awkwardly. As she fumbled,
her thumb dug into some slime. Hannah appeared to be
weeping, as if with some disease that had gone unnoticed.

Hetty wiped her thumb on the damp moss underfoot
and remained standing for a time, staring in disbelief at the
brown sickness oozing from the wound deep in Hannah's
heartwood.

Why These Dreams?

Hetty ached with a heavy sadness. Her hands felt unclean,
yet she knew washing them again would do no good.
Maybe tomorrow she would have the strength to face
Hannah's condition. Could it be heart rot? Tomorrow she
would tell Leaf about Hannah, but tonight she hoped for a
sound and dreamless sleep.

Years ago, feelings of guilt had caused frightening
nighttime images. She always counted on her covers
to provide protection against all the evils lurking in the
darkness. Now she tossed from side to side, pulling the
bedding over her head the way she had in her childhood.
But the patchwork quilt she had made with Mother offered

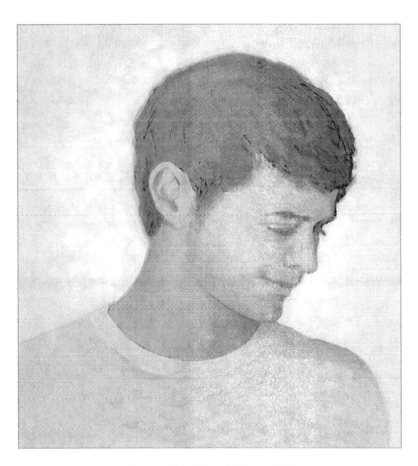

You want to deserve his friendship and his praise.

no comfort.

Hetty lay staring at a crack in the ceiling. In her mind it widened until, like Hannah's wound, it was oozing slime.

She had hoped to outgrow these nightmares. Finally her eyelids became heavy, but when sleep came at last, she thrashed in the clutches of a disturbing dream. In the dream, her hands were grasping Katrinka by the throat. Raspberry stains spread down the front of Katrinka's elegant lace dress, down her neck and upward into her hair. She was gasping for air.

When Hetty tried to remove her hands they closed tighter and tighter, and the raspberries became blood. She cried out for someone to pull her hands off before it was too late, but no one came.

The next minute she was in Hannah's branches holding a shriveled Katrinka. Tenderly, she cradled her limp body like a china doll, and cried, "I didn't mean to do it!" but even the night sky didn't believe her.

Darkness closed in on them, and Hannah's leaves whispered, "Hetty…. What have you done?" over and over. The old tree became so weak with sorrow and disappointment that her drooping leaves could no longer whisper.

"I didn't want to do it, Hannah! It was my hands that did it.

"I tried to love her.

"Oh, please Hannah, don't die!"

When Hetty awoke, the bed was damp with perspiration. Blackness crept toward her from the corners of the room and from under the closet door. The shadows now reached their fingers toward her, accusing her of dark thoughts.

Maybe the nightmare would stop if she turned on all the lights in her room, but she feared the dream would return if she closed her eyes again.

She had to think things through.

What good is it to pull the covers over my head? It's just hard to breathe.

These dreams.... They're not because of anything I've done. Could my thoughts be making these dreams?

I should never think the way I did about Katrinka. Not about anyone.

I need to think about something good instead. Like about Max and Mimi's anniversary. We'll be singing for them tomorrow.

CHAPTER EIGHT

Happy Anniversary

Max stood outside Mimi's dressing room, his knuckles poised to rap on her door. Today was their anniversary. All day he had been on the verge of saying something about it to her. It was already four in the afternoon, and he hadn't yet found the courage.

By doing nothing at all, he reasoned, their past and future commemorations could never suffer by comparison. So, as in years past, they had no plans to celebrate.

He clenched his jaw as regrets seethed in his memory.

We've usually made separate plans, but there's nothing on for tonight. If she were to answer my knock, what would I say?

Whatever happened to us? I can't remember any more. Maybe I just gave up when she listened to her father's opinion of me. I should have tried to prove him wrong, but no, I had to roll over and die. And she watched me do it. Drinking every night…stupid things like that.

Max withdrew to a deep leather chair, where he chose to brood alone.

After a few minutes of listening restlessly to his own breathing, he spoke firmly to himself. "Knock it off. You've never really failed till you stop trying."

He rested his chin on his fist.

Phil, my one true friend… I'm going to miss you. I can still hear you saying, "Don't look where you don't want to go." I should have taken your advice. It's not like I wanted to be a rich bum, but that's what I saw for myself, so that's what I've become.

How is it Morgan could put himself through law school, while I might not even graduate from Alcoholics Anonymous? He'll make it because of you, Phil. You were everything to Morgan that I should have been.

After all the mistakes I've made, Morgan and Melinda are getting it right. They watch Mimi and me, and they go make their own choices. Better ones.

Max looked across the trees to the gatehouse and scowled at the irritating chatter of birds outside the window. It's not that he was enjoying his misery. He was merely occupied with the memory of his friend.

Just as Phil had helped Max work things out when he was alive, maybe the memory of his wise advice would continue to make life better for all of them.

He glanced toward Mimi's door, and the hardness of his features seemed to soften a little. Was it with some unfamiliar hope or a glimpse of a better future?

The doorbell rang, interrupting his thoughts. Before the chimes had finished their melody, he said, "Drat," under his breath.

He heard Swenson open the front door to some callers. Who could be making this untimely visit? The voices of Hetty Lawrence and her father were the only two he recognized. Before he could figure out who was responsible for the rest of the commotion, Melinda ushered them upstairs somewhat sheepishly.

Normally Hetty was rather reserved, but Max noticed a glow of excitement about her. Behind Leaf came his wife Marian, holding their chubby redheaded baby.

Max was able to respond with courtesy in spite of his surprise. Hoping the baby wouldn't drool on the upholstery, he offered them all a seat.

Hetty spoke for the group. "Oh, no thank you," she said. "We've come to serenade you and Mimi for your anniversary." She seemed breathless with anticipation.

The baby reached out then squealed with laughter when Hetty took him from his mother. Leaf took out his violin and tuned it briefly.

Mimi's door squeaked open only two inches, but that was enough for Hetty, who cried, "Happy anniversary!" in the direction of the crack. The others joined in with slightly forced enthusiasm.

There was an awkward pause while Mimi seemed to consider disappearing behind the door. But whether curiosity or the requirements of good breeding, something made her widen the crack and step toward them.

The group erupted in song and were soon emboldened by each other's voices and the violin accompaniment. The baby laughed along with them, adding joy to the performance. Even Melinda's participation became more enthusiastic and spirited.

Max glanced at Mimi cautiously, trying to read her expression. Maybe she would bestow her approval upon the motley gathering. After all, her appearance of inflexible formality might be only that. He would have to wait and see before reacting on his own.

"No," he thought. "I'm going to enjoy it whether she does or not. Besides, who knows… maybe she's watching me the same way."

He decided that was exactly what Mimi was doing. When she showed a guarded gratitude for the friendly attention, Max thought it was probably his own acceptance that granted her permission.

Soon the violin became softer and the voices hummed, blending in a quiet and familiar melody. Even the baby became still, as if awaiting what might soon occur.

Hetty smiled and approached Max with a nod, as if to say, "It's you she's waiting to hear."

"No," he thought. "Mimi hasn't wanted me to sing for years."

The violin was playing "Some Enchanted Evening."

"She loved me once," he thought, "when she was young, before I carried her over the threshold. We used to laugh together. I was everything to her then."

He remembered her sweet breath, her graceful walk, and the many things they once promised to do together.

Max hoped he had nothing to lose by being bold. He wasn't too sure he knew the words to the song, but they would come to him. Once again he saw Mimi as his innocent young bride. Her smile was too much to hope for, but his eyes were on her when he dared.

Everything seemed to happen in slow motion. The fluid sound of his rich voice held the energy he had saved for twenty-five years, and his every word was charged with warmth.

The song came to its delicate end, like a silken thread that could snap or continue to dangle a broken heart.

Mimi's lips parted, and Max held his breath. As he drew

near, she pressed them firmly together. He was close enough to see the twitch in her left cheek and the confusion in her moist eyes. He could almost touch her, but she withdrew with a gasp and shut the door, returning to the shadows of her room.

Max stood facing the door in silent humiliation and allowed Melinda to show the party to the door. He couldn't face them. Their farewell wishes for a happy anniversary were a valiant effort to cheer him, yet their voices sounded empty and mechanical after such a disappointment.

Max had conflicting emotions, but didn't know what they were. Embarrassment? Anger? Love? Or maybe he didn't really care any more. Hetty had gone out of her way to do an act of kindness and had left looking crestfallen. The least he could do was to get to the bottom of it.

That door was not going to shut him out. He straightened his spine and turned the knob. Max Morganthal was through rolling over and playing dead!

There she was, lying on the chaise longue. Max hadn't expected to see the dignity of this icy woman so thoroughly dissolved in sobs. He was not actually certain she was crying, or even that she was capable of showing feelings of that sort.

As he stepped closer to discover whether she might be suffering from convulsions brought on by a sudden fever, she turned her red and swollen eyes toward him.

"You came," she whispered. Perhaps Mimi thought he was there to offer a long-awaited embrace. Reaching toward him, the open palms of her hands invited him to her side.

Max felt drained of his customary confidence and not at all sure what to do with his arms, having so little practice. Somehow, while attempting to control the beating of his heart, he muddled through without falling over her.

As Mimi smiled at him weakly, he tried unsuccessfully to stop the shaking of his hands.

Slowly she spoke the lines they both remembered from the opera *Vanessa*. Her voice was small and halting.

"Love has a bitter core," she said.

Max looked down at her hands and gripped them tightly. "Oh, please, Mimi, please don't stop there!" he thought. He held his breath and waited, hoping to hear the rest of the words.

There was a new look of turmoil in her eyes, but her voice was steady. *"Let me taste this bitterness with you,"* she said.

Trust

As they drove away, Hetty looked back. Melinda appeared reluctant to reenter her house. She lingered on the porch until they could no longer see her.

"Well," said Marian, "whatever their anniversary might have been, I think we just made it worse."

Leaf adjusted the rear view mirror with his long fingers and looked up to see Hetty's reflection. "Often things look a little better after a good sleep," he said.

Marian looked over her shoulder and nodded in agreement as if she loved the gentle tone of his voice.

"That's right," she said. "What's the worst that could happen? Maybe you won't be invited to their next anniversary celebration."

"I wasn't even invited to this one," said Hetty.

"After tonight they'll be uninviting us to the previous twenty-five as well," said Marian with a nervous cheerfulness.

Hetty tried to laugh. "I know they would," she said, "if there were any such thing as a retroactive uninvitation card."

She looked out the window. "I just don't want to get

uninvited to marry Morgan," she said.

"Was he busy tonight?" asked Marian.

"Yes. He's still working on the funeral with Katrinka." Hetty hesitated. "It's been about a week since I've seen him."

There was silence in the car until Leaf cleared his throat, probably in preparation for words of comfort, which he failed to produce.

Marian began optimistically in his place. "I think...I mean I'm sure ...." she said. Her voice tapered off, as she was apparently not so sure after all.

Hetty sighed. She was sure of one thing. Katrinka wanted more from Morgan than help with the funeral.

Little Danny squealed a few times and sucked his thumb noisily, as if none of this mattered.

Leaf slowed the car to read the signs ahead at the side of the road. They said, *No Parking Parade Route*, and *Parade Route Detour*. Apparently they concerned something that would happen in the future, so he resumed his earlier speed.

"Katrinka will miss her father," said Leaf. "Phil was a wise and good man."

Marian rummaged around for Danny's bottle. "I wouldn't sit back and watch her take over," she said. "You'd better put up a fight, Hetty." Leaf was silent.

Hetty heard the familiar crunch of gravel under the tires, signaling their arrival at her driveway. "If you'll come in," she said, "Mother and Papa will be waiting with some cookies."

Leaf glanced at Danny. "Another time," he whispered. "If he hears that 'c' word, your baby brother will never go to sleep."

Soon Hetty was sitting at the kitchen table.

"Did my namesake join in the singing?" asked Dan.

Hetty smiled. "Danny's a born star, Papa. They would

have brought him in just now, but Father thought he should be in bed."

Dora poured three glasses of milk and placed a cookie before each of them.

Hetty loved the little blue forget-me-nots around the rim of her plate. She traced them absently with her finger until Papa placed his hand on hers. She knew he could read and understand her concerns.

"He wasn't there, was he?" It was a statement, more than a question.

"No." She looked across the table and into his eyes. "Marian thinks I should put up a fight."

Papa said, "Marian sometimes has trouble trusting in people. Morgan's commitment to you has been long and consistent."

No matter what her papa might say, Hetty couldn't help wondering if Marian had a point. Dan saw the confusion in her eyes, and he began again. "What kind of relationship do you want with him?" he asked.

She stared at the seams in the wallpaper and waited for him to supply the answer, but it was clear he wanted her to fill in the blank herself. She thought, "Papa wants me to choose between being trusting or suspicious."

Her papa's cookie broke and crumbled onto the table. He said, "I know Morgan has to deal with constant flirtation from girls." He paused to honk his nose into a large red handkerchief. "It happens enough that it can't be easy for him," he said. "It requires a lot of diplomacy on his part."

Hetty looked down again at the little blue flowers. Papa's words weren't particularly comforting, but she tried to appreciate his directness.

Dan looked into Hetty's somber face and grinned broadly. "You know what I think?" he said. "Whatever qualities people have, that's what they care about. People who are kind and thoughtful look for those same traits in a mate."

Hetty thought he could be right. But maybe that was a reason for handsome people to be drawn to beauty. There was the maxim, *birds of a feather flock together*. If true, she was convinced Mother Nature had been tragically unfair to her. Frequently, Hetty heard it said that Morgan and Katrinka made the most beautiful couple in recent memory.

Dora perched on the edge of her chair to add a thought. "I'm sure Morgan was glad you sang for his parents," she said.

"If so, then he's the only person who was," said Hetty. "I embarrassed everyone."

Dora stroked Hetty's soft hair back from her forehead. "I love the way you did it anyway," she said. "You were right to take a chance."

The Morning News

Hetty slept poorly another night. Hannah's sickness was still on her mind, and she had dreams of the magnificent tree calling to her in agony. Thinking there must surely be something her father could do, she had gone to Leaf with her worries.

Now it was morning, and she hoped he might come with a good report. Half awake, Hetty lay in bed in foggy drowsiness, awaiting the news.

The front doorbell rang, and Hetty heard Mother and Papa at the front door. "By all means," said Dora. "Hetty will be delighted to have you wake her up."

It was not Leaf, but Hetty was happy to hear Melinda's voice. She lay with her eyes half closed and waited for her friend to tiptoe in.

Soon Melinda sat on the edge of the bed and whispered,

"Hetty, you won't believe it." She moved Hetty's hair away from her ear.

"I couldn't wait to tell you… Dad went down to the kitchen this morning in his robe and made breakfast for Mom. I saw when he went past my door. He even put a red rose in a bud vase!"

Hetty's eyes opened wide, and she sat up straight in bed. It was absolutely delicious to hear the joy in Melinda's voice. "I never would have expected it," said Melinda. "Not after last night. He carried the tray upstairs to her and then they closed the door."

Hetty waited for her to report Morgan's reaction. When there was no mention of his response, disappointment dampened some of Hetty's excitement. Maybe he didn't know about it because he wasn't there? She tried to smile. Realizing it was useless to worry about Morgan right now, she resolved to enjoy the good news.

Melinda leaned closer. "I'll tell you the best thing of all," she said. "Dad was humming "Ah, Sweet Mystery of Life" under his breath." She flopped back on the bed and laughed, landing on the lumpiness of Hetty's long legs.

Moments later, Melinda stood beside the bed to signal the opening of a new subject. "There's something else," she said. "But the main thing is, well…. Please don't worry about what's printed in the paper. Whatever you read, I'm sure it couldn't have come from Morgan."

"What do you mean?" asked Hetty.

"Well, I wanted to tell you myself, before you saw it." Melinda reached in her bag and pulled out the morning paper. "You know Katrinka does pretty much as she wishes," she said, "and I suppose Morgan doesn't want to be too blunt with her right now."

She smoothed the quilt over Hetty's feet and explained further. "The way I see it, Tilly Teller knows Katrinka's alone in the world. And she figures Morgan must be a great comfort to her."

Melinda took a deep breath. "Besides, she must think that big diamond ring makes a great story," she said. "Who wouldn't?"

Hetty knew the ring normally dangled luxuriously from a gold chain around Katrinka's neck. Except for when she retrieved it from deep inside her neckline, to the admiration of all who requested that she do so.

Melinda dropped the topic of the "Tilly Tells All" gossip column and opened a new subject. "Here's what else I know," she said. "This is the biggest news of all. And it won't even be in the paper." Melinda made her famous bug-eyed face, which she reserved for exceptional declarations.

"Believe it or not, Katrinka actually wants to honor her father with a circus event," she said. "Dad told her he'd pay for any kind of funeral she wanted, and she's chosen to have a parade with elephants!"

Hetty blinked in surprise. Katrinka always refused to have anything to do with "those smelly animals." In contrast, Hetty had loved working with Morgan to care for the elephants. Her interest in them and love for the circus had brought her closer to him.

Even the public saw Katrinka's disdain for the circus as dampening her fairy tale romance with Morgan. But now it appeared Katrinka had changed her attitude dramatically.

Melinda continued eagerly. "Morgan spent the week reaching some of the circus people Phil and Dad used to know. Like clowns and others who admired Phil. They'll be coming out of retirement. It's supposed to be a surprise, but Dad said I could tell you about it."

There was a long pause. Melinda seemed to be gathering her courage to discuss one more thing.

"Would you forgive me if I didn't go to the class reunion

with you?" she asked quietly.

"Of course," said Hetty. "Has something come up?"

A sheepish smile came to Melinda's face. "It's Dart," she said. "I'm so sorry. I don't dare turn down an invitation from him." She sighed. "Maybe nothing special will come of it, but I wish it would." Her cheeks colored.

Hetty did not want to take the train without Melinda, who was a more confident traveler, but she did her best to put on a cheerful face. She could only hope Melinda's time with Dart would be worthwhile. In the past, the reunions had been at the Haxton School. This one would be near the city where the organizers lived.

"I hope you'll still go to the reunion without me," said Melinda. "Morgan will be leaving town in two days anyway, you know."

Hetty had not known.

Melinda looked toward the ceiling. "I'm trying to think if there's anything else I was supposed to tell you." At first nothing seemed to come to her mind, but as she prepared to leave, she recalled what it was. "Oh, I remember. Morgan says he'll be going to the designers' convention. He has to represent L.C. Cosmetics."

Hetty clenched her fist and asked, "Does Katrinka have to go too?" She tried to sound unconcerned. "I was just wondering, now that she's working for L.C. too." Her heart was in her throat, and she thought to herself, "Please say Katrinka won't be there with Morgan!"

Melinda's answer was slow in coming. "No," she said, "Katrinka doesn't have to go. But she wants to, so the company's paying her way. It's probably lucky, since Morgan knows absolutely zero about cosmetics."

She smiled at Hetty. "I'll admit I'm honestly relieved to know she's going, so she'll be away from Dart," she said. "Thanks for your concern. I know that's why you asked."

Melinda thought of something else. "Tilly Teller's going too," she said. "She and Katrinka are good friends now. Since Phil began to fail, Tilly's been spending more time with her."

She sighed. "I ought to be happy for Katrinka. She has the perfect face to represent the company, and she knows it. I hope this trip will help her recover. Phil's death broke her heart."

Melinda used the newspaper to tap Hetty affectionately on the head. After a cheerful apology she was gone.

Stunned, Hetty stared at the ceiling.

CHAPTER NINE

Ignoring the Morning News

The offending newspaper article was still lying on Hetty's pillow where Melinda had left it moments ago. As if to demand her attention, the paper unfurled against her face of its own accord, and for a time Hetty lay with her nose to what seemed to be Morgan's picture.

It was close enough to her eyes that it was only a blur. That was just fine with her. Hetty closed her eyes. "I don't want to think about it or do anything," she thought. She pulled the sheet over her face.

The morning sounds, normally so pleasing to her, felt disturbing. It was entirely because of the unsettling news from Melinda. As the muffled voices of Mother and Papa reached her through the door, she chose to remain in the familiar setting of her own bedroom.

Dora was clattering dishes. Hetty knew her mother would soon place the bacon in the cast iron pan to sizzle. She tried to picture how the sun must be shining through the kitchen window just now and the way it filled the room with brilliant light. She could picture it spilling over the flowered tablecloth and the little china saucers with their forget-me-nots.

The last teacup had been broken while she was away at college. Hetty couldn't bear to think of how the little cup might have come to its end. Maybe Papa bumped it with his elbow when he pulled his handkerchief from his pocket, and it broke into a hundred tiny shards.

They couldn't have realized every last piece was a treasure deserving gratitude for dear memories. Especially the pieces decorated with hand-painted flowers. How could they have known?

Hetty sighed. "I don't want to go to the reunion," she whispered to herself.

She decided to fill her mind with thoughts of carefree times around the kitchen table; evenings with Mother and Papa, before her heart operation. So many ideas had happened there as they played with the magic of language, writing limericks and inventing ridiculous words.

And the Ovaltine. They often sipped hot Ovaltine or cocoa from the china cups. Even now, she could feel the little painted forget-me-nots under the light touch of her fingers.

Hetty could still hear her mother singing off key while Papa listened to her affectionately. The family had felt complete.

Then they found Leaf, her father. Marian joined them several years later, and they all delighted in their shared affection. Hetty had thrived in the increased wholeness of her family. Surely they would all understand her need to stay home.

It would be pleasant to return to those simpler times. But it could never happen now, because the meaning of the word *wholeness* had been turned upside down.

It now meant being with Morgan.

Hetty thought of the many times she had poured out her heart to Hannah, the mother-tree. She had marveled when the immense boughs swayed as if in response to her private thoughts and emotions. High in Hannah's lacy canopy of leaves, she felt loved and nurtured. And Hannah had given her the courage to reach for Morgan.

The massive oak had seemed immortal then.

With the hem of her sheet, Hetty wiped away a tear.

She spread the newspaper flat and cupped her chin in the other hand. Tilly Teller's article covered the entire half page. The heading said, *Together Again.*

The beautiful pictures of Morgan and Katrinka side by side took her breath away. Under the photographs were the words, *Beauty and the Best.*

Morgan's eyes looked real and alive. His earnest and sober expression spoke to Hetty of courage and revived in her the memory of a discussion they once had about fear.

Morgan said whenever he was dropped at the scene of a forest fire, his confidence depended on how well he had prepared. If his parachute was packed properly and he carried the right equipment, his eagerness to protect the forest was stronger than his fear of the fire.

Hetty told herself to prepare so she could conquer her fears. She repeated the idea to herself over and over.

What I need is courage, but how can I prepare against Katrinka? She's my fear.

I can't confront her. Phil asked me to be her friend.

Her friend. . . . Maybe that's the key. I should concentrate on what to be, more than what to do.

Papa was right. It's not in my nature to fight for Morgan.

The way to get rid of an enemy is to turn her into a friend.

Still, maybe I do have weapons. Love and trust. I suppose they're the two best weapons I have.

Here's what I'll do…. I'll throw out the paper without reading the article.

I have better things to do.

She rose quickly from her bed, vigorously crumpled the morning paper into the wastebasket, and gathered the unruly puffs of her hair into a blue satin ribbon. Straightening her spine, she addressed her image in the mirror.

"Love Katrinka," she said. "And trust Morgan."

Flaky

On the morning of the funeral, the telephone rang. It was Marian. "Hetty," she said, "I'd love your advice.

"I chopped the rhubarb and put it in the pie tin. Then I had to take it out again because I didn't have the piecrust made yet! It's just that I was in a hurry because the kitchen was so hot. It seems like I've had the oven on for *hours*," she said. "You can't just slip a pie crust under the filling. The crust is the part I haven't figured out yet."

"Doesn't Father normally make the pies?"

"Yes," said Marian, "but he's gone to look at Hannah again. This time he's taken a friend with him. A tree surgeon. They'll see what they can do. Hetty, just so you know…it doesn't look good. Please don't get your hopes up about Hannah."

"I can't help it," said Hetty. "I know Hannah's sicker than we thought at first, but I can't let myself think that way. Now what about the pie?" she asked.

Marian took a big breath. "Well, the recipe says to add four tablespoons of ice water," she said. "So are they talking about heaping tablespoons or flat ones?"

Hetty hesitated. "Heaping? What do you mean?"

"I'm wondering about the surface tension," said Marian, "...the way it sort of piles up on the tablespoon."

"That's a good question, Marian," she said, not entirely convinced that it was. "But piecrusts aren't that fussy. That's why they say, *easy as pie*. The main thing is you shouldn't handle it too much, or it might get tough."

"What do you mean, tough?" asked Marian.

"Well...cardboardy," said Hetty. "You want it to be flaky."

"I do? It mostly looks crumbly."

Hetty explained she was referring to the end results.

Marian brightened. "You mean not like boot leather," she said.

"Right," said Hetty. "That's exactly how you don't want it."

A little later, Marian called. "Well, I tasted the pie," she said. "Have I told you what my stepfather Joey and I did once? We sucked the centers out of a box of chocolate creams. It was our best April fool's trick ever.

"Anyway, the pie smelled so good," said Marian, "I had to try it. I sucked it out of a slit in the top crust. Isn't fruit supposed to be sweet?" she said. "It's completely inedible. Maybe I shouldn't have left out the sugar."

"Don't toss it out," said Hetty. "You remember the Haxton School motto? *I shall find a way or make one.* Morgan says sometimes you have to *find a way or* fake *one*."

"How would you do that?"

"There's no law that says you have to call it *pie*," said Hetty. "Pretend it's cobbler. Maybe add some extra sugar to vanilla pudding and pour it over the rhubarb. Give it a fancy name."

"What would I do without you?" said Marian. "They ought to put *you* in headlines." She stopped to think. *"How about, Hetty the Homemaker Invents Rhubarb Rapture!"*

Hetty understood why Marian mentioned headlines. She'd seen the Tilly Teller article. If Marian saw it, so did everyone else.

There was a crash on the other end of the telephone, and Hetty was relieved to learn it was just a broken lamp, not the baby.

Marian gasped. "What next!" she said. "It's not just the lamp. Danny dumped flour on the floor and now he's crawled across the carpet. Leaf is due to bring his friend here any second. I don't know what to do," said Marian. "Guess I'll lie next to the vacuum in a tragic faint. That's about all I can do."

Hetty laughed. "Father's friend isn't coming to see your floors," she said. "He's coming to meet you and Danny. Try not to worry about things you can't fix. Father will appreciate your *trying* to make a pie, but he'll be even happier to know you're not stuck to the freezer this time."

"Oh, Hetty! This place is a disaster, and I only have two hands. What would you do?"

"What would I do?" Hetty felt a lump in her throat. Quietly, she said, "I would...I would use them both for holding Danny very close."

Hetty heard a car on the gravel driveway. Melinda had come for her. "We'll talk later," she said. "And Marian.... I love you for making me feel useful. How did you know that was what I needed most?

"If you and Father have to miss the parade," she added, "I'll tell you all about it when I get back from the reunion."

"Thanks, but my brother Joseph can give us a report," said Marian. "He always hangs around Katrinka in case she wants his listening ear. Maybe they're just friends, but Joseph will be there even if she doesn't notice."

*Danny dumped flour on the floor and
now he's crawled across the carpet.*

It wasn't easy for Hetty to greet Melinda with a smile. The beautiful faces of Morgan and Katrinka were still emblazoned in her memory. She could picture the large letters below them: *Beauty and the Best.*

If only she could pour out her heart to Hannah! Hetty wondered how long she could hope to feel the warmth of Hannah's branches. How much time was left for the magnificent oak?

The Funeral

Never had the street felt as empty as it did now. Hetty and Melinda found a low railing close to the curb and sat back against it to await the funeral cortège. The somewhat eerie nothingness was all the more exaggerated in contrast with the bustling traffic normally expected at this time of the morning.

Groups of families and friends trickled in along the sidewalk, slowly at first. Gradually, people clustered in reverent stillness. Then like honey that finally passes the neck of the jar, the crowd came in a sudden large swell. They all quietly melted into the scene to seek places to sit or stand.

Hetty heard two men speaking in low tones behind her.

"How did you hear about this?" said the one.

"I didn't," came the answer. "But seeing that elephant last night...figured it had to do with Phil." The other whistled under his breath and shuffled his feet.

Someone next to them volunteered more information. "It's gotta be Morganthal money paying for it," he said. "They were friends, you know."

"Right," said another, "and the Morganthal boy's

marrying Phil's daughter."

"It's about time."

Melinda rolled her eyes for Hetty's benefit then pointed out a sign on the glass door behind them. It said, "Whittlesey's Drug Store will remain closed until noon to honor the memory of Phil Wallace." Melinda looked in the window and returned a smile to the soda jerk who nodded to her from behind the counter.

"The merchants along here offered to open late," said Melinda, "before Morgan even asked them."

Without any warning, around the corner they came. There was no fanfare, drum roll, or music of any sort. The first to appear in silent tribute was a man wearing a tall red silk hat and holding a trumpet. Melinda gripped Hetty's arm with excitement. "He was ringmaster when I was little!" she said.

Nearby, a small girl squealed with excitement. Her father whispered rules of behavior before lifting her to his shoulders.

Next came a full brass band dressed in red and gold. They marched slowly and silently to some subtle signal from the drum major. With every movement the instruments flashed in the sun.

The absence of ordinary sound made it increasingly apparent something grand was missing. The rustling fabric of the bright banners could not satisfy the expectations of hearing. Uncle Sam, walking in slow motion on his stilts, could not compensate for the silence.

The crowd understood the message. There was a certain emptiness that had happened with the passing of Phil Wallace.

Whispers came in snatches from every direction:

"Did I ever tell you about when my sister broke her leg? Yeah, Phil got her laughing so hard she forgot she'd never dance again."

"You suppose he was so smart because…you know how his head was kind of big? I mean are dwarfs smarter than regular people?"

"I'm sure I knew him before you did."

"Didn't you know? He was an advocate for humane treatment of elephants. Lectured all over."

"Did he ever get his book finished?"

"He showed me pictures of his daughter. You never saw anyone so proud."

"She's a beauty queen, you know."

"Mostly I came to see Morgan. My sister has a crush on him."

Her companion giggled. "Who doesn't?"

The circus had been an important part of Melinda's early years. Hetty wondered if her friend would prefer to be with Dart so she could explain some of the interesting things she knew.

Suddenly Hetty noticed Dart nearby in the crowd and was glad she hadn't asked Melinda about him. He seemed aware of the two of them, yet it appeared he wanted to see the parade alone. Maybe Dart didn't want anything to interfere with his watching for Katrinka.

All eyes strained to see what else might come around the corner. Surely, the elephants would be next.

Instead, a tall red-nosed clown appeared. His bushy orange hair bounced with every step of his long, floppy shoes. With each turn of his head, they could see a big tear painted on one cheek. His white-gloved hands pulled a little red and blue striped wagon slowly behind him. Each time he neared the crowds at the side of the road, he bowed toward the wagon.

Melinda stared in disbelief. "Hetty," she whispered, "it's my dad."

In the wagon was the brightly colored clown costume Phil had so often worn. His tall green hat wobbled ridiculously on top of the carefully folded clothes. Max turned frequently to look back at the little wagon, gesturing as if to communicate with its contents. The tender emotions he expressed in pantomime conveyed his sorrow.

His partnership with Phil was now over. Slowly each finger of his white gloves moved to somehow communicate his disbelief. Holding the costume high before him, with a tilt of his head, Max seemed to plead with the limp cloth.

A sweet surge of sentiment stirred the eager crowd with childlike expectations: perhaps the costume would once again move the way it did when Phil occupied it. For a moment, the living form of Phil seemed almost visible to the silent gathering.

A little boy looked at the small costume and broke the silence. "I didn't know he was short," he said.

The child had expressed the unspoken thoughts of the crowd. Phil Wallace had the flesh and bones of a dwarf, yet in life he pushed the boundaries of his diminutive body. Now in death the impact of his big heart and soul seemed all the more expansive.

Down the street on the other side, Hetty saw a woman on a white wooden lawn chair. She wore a graceful, flowing skirt and a yellow broad-brimmed hat. All eyes were on the tall clown as he approached the woman. Bowing deeply before her, he doffed his hat with ceremony.

Melinda gasped. "That's Mom!" she said.

The crowd watched the woman extend her hand and reach toward the clown, inviting him closer. Her eyes shone with happiness as Max kissed her fingers. She seemed unaware of the audible sigh arising from the crowd.

Max turned from her to display his dramatically pounding heart. Melinda laughed softly. "The tube goes up inside his shirt," she said, "and when he squeezes the bulb...." Her whispers tapered off, but she was smiling broadly.

Silence reigned throughout the performance. It continued as Max once again drew attention to the contents of the wagon and disappeared around the bend, making room for the rest of the cortège to follow.

Bereaved Beauty

The elephants came in single file, each baby's trunk holding onto the tail of the bigger one in front. The only sound was the mysterious low rumble of their occasional communications.

"Here she comes," said Melinda. Hetty wondered who she meant. There was no sign of Katrinka.

"That's Lulu," said Melinda. "I knew she'd be first."

Hetty had heard of Lulu. "Wasn't she Blossom's allomother?" she asked.

Melinda stretched forward to get a better view of the elephant. "Yes," she said. "When Blossom and her mother were separated, Lulu nursed her. Dad's still trying to reunite them. Now that we don't own them, we don't have much say in the matter. That could change, though."

Melinda sat back against the railing. "I ought to tell you something that's happened," she said. "Yesterday, my parents gave up all their liquid assets. Basically, all their money. Of course they still have the businesses that are doing really well. And they'll always take care of Katrinka.... But you know that whole story."

Hetty thought it best not to appear surprised or show any reaction.

Melinda cleared her throat and continued. "Anyway, they've put every last penny into establishing an elephant sanctuary in Phil's name. Dad won't stand by and see elephants butchered for their tusks," she said. "Poaching is serious, you know. They really could become extinct because people are so greedy for ivory.

"They need a lot of space, too. And the way elephants bond for life, they shouldn't be separated...especially the females. It's too cruel."

Hetty directed her gaze up the street where she was most likely to see Morgan at any moment, but a huge old bull elephant came next. Melinda knew this one, too.

"They say Tembo was hard to train, but he's smart," she said. "He's about sixty years old now, and more docile. Tembo's the Swahili word for *elephant*. It means *boy*, too."

Always moving slowly, his trunk sometimes swinging from side to side, Tembo carried Phil's casket on his back. It was a simple pine casket of ordinary workmanship, just as he had requested. Poppies and purple iris decorated the space under the casket on the sides, obscuring the substantial straps that held it in place. A spray of roses covered the lid.

Tembo's sunken temples spoke of wisdom and untold memories. A blaze of red satin and gold braid decorated his great head. Each time he raised and lowered his massive padded feet, multiple rows of bells turned and flipped along his entire length. But they made no sound. Red silk tassels had been carefully secured onto the many clappers to silence them.

The elephants moved on. Because there was not the recent memory of clatter to compare it with, the silence of their soft padded feet left a far greater impression.

Hetty decided commotion seems greatest when

reflecting back on it, as it dwindles. Once it has died down to a fragile memory, it takes a moment to be sure of the change. Only then can the ghost of it announce, "So this is what silence sounds like!"

When a chirping sparrow broke the silence, the faces of the crowd turned toward it as if to say, "Oh, we'd completely forgotten about noise!"

To Hetty, the silence was all the more grand because she knew Katrinka's arrival would dispel it. She watched for her, wondering how she would present herself.

Katrinka always has to play beauty queen and make sure all eyes are on her. When she comes, she'll act like she's "Miss this or Miss that," waving and blowing kisses. Maybe she'll be in a convertible. Morgan could even be driving it. All I know for sure is she won't go anywhere near the animals.

She'll be dressed in pink and wear her hair waving over one eye. The other will be kept free for winking at anything over eighteen in trousers.

For a space of two minutes, the crowd seemed restless. They whispered questions and watched for what might come next.

There were more low rumblings from the elephants. Then she came.

Katrinka was seated behind the ears of an average-sized female elephant. It had a simple covering over its back, though its head was adorned in a style similar to Tembo's. They approached slowly.

Maybe some new sensitivity had inspired Katrinka to understand the dignity that was required. Hetty thought she had never seen a more beautiful woman. There was a graceful simplicity about her demeanor.

The awe Hetty felt at the sight made the air escape from her lungs. Tripping on the laces of her own boots, she lurched forward and stumbled against the woman in front of her.

Katrinka's eyes were on the casket not too far ahead. Not in the least fearful, her serenity was consistent with the atmosphere of decorum. When the elephant raised its trunk high, there was no change in Katrinka's expression, and she remained steady.

But Hetty saw her turn pale and glance briefly at someone on the ground. A man was there to offer reassurance. He was attentive and watchful. Hetty wondered why she hadn't noticed him earlier.

Maybe it was because he was dressed like a canvasman. He could have been anyone, but to Katrinka he was all that mattered. The man was Morgan.

With astonishing clarity, Hetty saw Katrinka passing an essential test. The absence of the usual heavy makeup seemed to reveal a woman who had made a change in her life. It was a change Morgan would like.

Everything symbolic of Katrinka's insincerity and unnatural ways seemed to have fallen away. Where were her false eyelashes? Her simple hairstyle spoke of a sweetness Hetty never expected to see. Even her dimples were at rest.

There were others milling about, but Katrinka's eyes were on no one but Morgan. She gripped the support as he directed. He was never out of her sight.

Hetty noticed the unspoken communications between them as they passed nearby, and she watched as Katrinka blushed almost imperceptibly. Since the two of them had shared experiences planning the funeral, the secret mystery of their private glances stung Hetty deeply.

Hetty felt dowdy in her wrinkled blouse, and tucked it in on the side where it had pulled out of her skirt. She reached down to lace her boots, but gave it up, realizing Morgan couldn't possibly see her feet in the crowd. Not that he was looking, anyway.

"What could he possibly see in me?" she thought.

Melinda attempted a wan smile. "Well, it's obvious who he cares about," she said. "I probably should have planned on the reunion after all. See over there?" she said. "He looks sort of hypnotized." She was watching Dart.

She soon brightened a little and said, "Let me drive you to the station."

"Thanks," said Hetty. "I'm already packed."

Hetty tried to quell her discomfort over traveling alone, but it was hard to stop fearing the many things that could go wrong and probably would. If only she didn't keep getting lost!

Hetty had learned when people said, "You can't miss it," she probably would. And the expression, "You can't get there from here," applied to her all too often.

"Papa was right," she thought. "I need to get over my fears. That's reason enough for me to go.

"And maybe it's a good idea to be away from Morgan."

CHAPTER TEN

The Train Trip

Hetty had forgotten to take her sweater to the train station, but when Melinda dropped her off, she gave Hetty the one she was wearing, to use on the trip. It would come in handy later. But for now Hetty placed it carefully folded behind her back and looked out the train window.

She leaned against the armrest and watched the ever-changing view as it blurred with unnerving speed. A lazy dog lay stretched out in the afternoon sun. It seemed to take no interest in the train.

Hetty sighed and let her mind wander.

Why don't dogs chase trains the way they chase cars? Their chances of catching one are just as good. Their sense of specific responsibility, I guess. No matter how far they run, I don't suppose dogs get lost.

The nice thing about sitting on the train...I won't get lost either. That is if I'm on the right one, going where it's supposed to.

Just to be sure, Hetty pulled out her ticket to check it once more, then put it away securely so it wouldn't get lost. When she had paid for it back at the station, she asked the man as many questions as she dared. He glared at her and said, "Look, Miss, it ain't that hard. Any idiot can figure it out."

Hetty pushed her suitcases farther under the seat and returned to her thinking.

I don't have it figured out, so that means I'm not an idiot. I just need more practice with traveling, I suppose. Papa thinks I'd have a better sense of direction if I hadn't been home schooled. While I was sick, the other children were walking to school and developing that instinct.

It sounds like Melinda will teach me to drive when I get back. That should help me be more independent. I don't want Morgan to think I'm a big baby. That is if he thinks of me at all.

Maybe it's Katrinka who's on his mind now.

Melinda will tell me about Phil's burial, but she's always careful what she says about Katrinka. Is it because she thinks Katrinka could become her sister-in-law?

The conductor interrupted her thoughts to ask for the ticket. She had put it somewhere in her purse. Or was it in a pocket? Where had she put it!

The lady next to her appeared never to have lost anything. With her mouth open, she watched Hetty drop a few scraps of paper and her lace handkerchief while searching the floor. Hetty tried not to dislike her.

When at last Hetty presented the ticket to the conductor and he punched it, the lady closed her mouth and smiled at her.

"Maybe she kept her mouth open as a way of helping me," thought Hetty. "It's like when Papa used to chew his tongue at the corner of his mouth while he watched me carve a pumpkin. But in the end, it's the smile that helps most."

Hetty clutched the ticket stub tightly, in case it would be needed again.

She still had a lot to work out in her mind and spent some time on how to control her thoughts about people. Especially Katrinka.

I'm sure Morgan expects me to feel understanding and forgiving. How could he want me if I'm guilty of ugly feelings?

Phil's face keeps coming up in my mind asking me to be Katrinka's friend. When I get back home, I should try. Maybe I need to tell her how I felt about the beautiful tribute today. Her father would have loved the way she honored his memory. She and Morgan.

Hetty resolved to think of ways to become someone Morgan would be proud to know. Her own person. Confident, with an air of independent maturity.

She thought uncertainly of the future.

Maybe someday I'll be coming home from a long day serving on the bench. I'll get into my large car, which I will have parked with precision and skill, in a space marked, Reserved for Judge Henrietta Lawrence. Violators will be towed at their own expense.

Morgan will be walking through the parking lot holding a small child. When he sees me, he will come show me his beautiful daughter. I will tell him she looks just like Katrinka must have looked at that age. He will ask my advice about how to deal with the court system in California, because Katrinka isn't receiving the proceeds from her last movie.

I won't tell him I know she's spent all the Morganthal money they inherited.

She was the star of the movie, yet there is some ongoing

dispute they can't resolve without interference from higher up the ladder. I will go to my car and radio the governor and the film studio, upon which the matter will be immediately resolved.

Morgan will thank me and tell me he felt sure I could do something due to my stature. I will tell him it's my pleasure to be of any assistance, and would he please give my love to Katrinka?

His little girl blows me a kiss, and Morgan looks at her tenderly with his dark blue eyes. When she hugs him around the neck with her chubby dimpled arms, he takes care not to scratch her with his dark whiskers. His beard is growing thick, as happens every evening about this time.

I say goodbye and sit in the car hoping no one can see me behind my dark glasses.

That night I cry myself to sleep, and not even two chocolate bars with toffee bits can make me forget how I love him; how I would give all I have and all I know, just to be whatever he wants me to be.

I'll try not to think about his gentle voice, his kind heart. I'll try to forget how the sun shines more brightly when I'm near him. I won't imagine his hand guiding me upward. Always up and into whatever is brighter and more wonderful.

He's good and true. Please love him well, Katrinka!

Hetty shivered and took her handkerchief from her purse, but put it away again when she remembered having dropped it on the floor. With the back of her hand, she wiped away a tear.

When the conductor announced Hetty's stop, she gathered her bags and smiled in the direction of the lady whose mouth was now closed, but she was asleep. Hetty was wishing she could be that much at ease.

Out on the platform, Hetty glanced in every direction.

Some of the signs threatened to be confusing if followed. Others promised to be equally confusing if *not* followed. But Hetty's little square overnight case made a good seat from which to consider the alternatives.

If only she had dared awaken the sleeping lady! She was almost like a friend now, and she might have suggested what to do next.

It seemed like no time at all before the last noisy "All aboard!" was called. Then Hetty remembered she had left Melinda's sweater on the seat. There wasn't a spare moment to gather her thoughts, let alone her luggage.

The conductor grumbled as she reentered, but Hetty moved quickly between the passengers, who jostled and adjusted their belongings. The lady was waiting for her. Peering through the crowd, she stood waving Melinda's sweater overhead.

One grateful smile later, Hetty had made her way past the growling conductor and back out onto the platform, before the train began to roll forward. There should be ample time to find the next train headed for the reunion. Hetty went directly to the place she'd left her suitcases.

They were not where she thought she had left them. Had she gotten off on the wrong side of the train? She waited for it to pull out of the station so she could see across the track. No suitcases.

She thought of her mother's confidence. The last thing her mother Dora had said was, "People are basically good and want to be helpful. Just have fun and ask for help when you need it."

I should have learned more from her. Here's what she would do. She'd go up to a perfect stranger and say, "Kind sir, where do you suppose I might have left my suitcases?"

And he would say, "I don't know, dear Lady, but may I

*suggest you be more careful whom you approach in the future? I
fear a thief or some other unsavory ruffian may have filched them.*

*"In fact, you see, in my daily life I am actually a vicious
ax murderer. But because you are so sweet and trusting, I shall
search the entire station to help you locate your luggage, setting
aside my plans for brutally disposing of you."*

In the ladies' room mirror Hetty saw her eyes were red
and her cheeks had pink splotches. After she splashed her
face with cold water, at least her cheeks were no longer
tearstained.

The hair around her face was a little wet and stringy,
but the ribbon she needed to hold it back was gone with
the stolen overnight case along with everything else.

Once again the tears overflowed.

Replacing Sabrina

At the far end of the train station, Rose Di Milano
approached her grim-faced husband, who guarded a wide
array of leather suitcases and trunks. On each piece of
luggage was a brass plate with the engraving, "Di Milano
Designer Fabrics."

Marco Di Milano had been waiting for his wife for
some time now and seemed relieved when she came from
behind to tug on his sleeve. "Ah, there you are.... Where
are the others?" he asked.

"We may have a solution," she said bravely.

He rolled his eyes. "Oh? Did Sabrina decide to come,
after all?" he said. "We can't keep forgiving all these last
minute cancellations of hers. The clothes look great on her,
but I'd rather hang them on a bean pole."

"I agree, hon," she said. "In fact I may have found just

the bean pole you're looking for." Rose smiled and looked through the crowds at Hetty. The Di Milano employees surrounded her and were speaking with animation.

"Do you remember Hetty Lawrence?" said Rose.

"No…. Unless she's the one who swept the spelling contest years ago."

"She's the one. A sweet child. Went to Haxton," she said, "…in the class between our two girls. I haven't set up anything definite with her. She knows I have to discuss it with you first."

"Mind you," said Marco, "it's not brains we're looking for here."

"True," said Rose, "but there couldn't be a model with fewer brains than Sabrina, and where did that get us?"

Marco appeared to fear what his wife was thinking. "Well, I guess," he mumbled.

Rose wasn't through.

"The poor little thing," she said. "Her luggage was stolen on the way to a Haxton class reunion, and she was beside herself. I think she was relieved to find a familiar face. I couldn't just leave her there like that. She remembers our girls, you know."

He stopped her and said, "It's not that I'm against helping her out…."

Rose continued. "Another thing," she said. "Hetty would be willing to go to the convention," she said, "because she has some connection with Morgan Morganthal."

"Connection? Really?" he said. "I knew he was coming. Of course, knowing the circles he moves in, I doubt he knows her well. But that's nice."

After spotting Hetty through the thinning crowd, Marco laughed nervously. "Does she seem a bit frumpy? I can't tell behind all that hair. About the same size as Sabrina, with a few alterations. Good bones…. A little taller, maybe?"

"Trust me," said Rose. "Have I ever been wrong?"

Marco answered that with just a smile.

He paused briefly. "Remember how long it took when we were coaching Sabrina? You can't turn an ugly duckling into a swan overnight."

Rose gave him an affectionate poke in the ribs. "I know," she said. "Aren't you glad we have forty-eight hours?"

Her words made him stare in space. "She'll need a complete going-over," he said.

Rose faced her husband with a look of gratitude. "There's something about Hetty," she said. "I think it's her innocence shining through. We're all going to love working with her. I promise you won't be sorry."

I Can't Bear the Guilt

As Morgan stepped into the banquet hall he was blinded briefly by the flash of a camera close to his face. The cameraman tipped his hat and sauntered away to seek another celebrity. Morgan wished he could bring Hetty to places like this. The time would pass more quickly with her by his side.

"But maybe it wouldn't be such a good idea anyway," he thought. "My dear Hetty…she'd feel so out of place here." He smiled. "I think she's uncomfortable in this kind of environment with all the glitter.

"She's most at home in the woods. We'll be happy together in the cottage, but we may need to lead separate lives sometimes."

An usher offered to show him to his table, but he wasn't ready to be seated. For now, there were too many hands to shake and friends he needed to acknowledge with a word or two.

Inside the portal to his left, Morgan heard a commotion and turned to discover the cause of it. A crowd had gathered to watch a tall young woman of regal bearing and appearance.

She moved with grace through the crowd, surrounded by a cadre of men and women protecting her from admirers and photographers. A crush of reporters followed her to the center of the hall and continued asking questions of her entourage. The young woman appeared to be grateful when those escorting her asked the crowd to give her some space.

Otherwise oblivious to the attention she had stirred, she gazed in all directions, as if searching for someone important to her.

"Who could she be looking for?" wondered Morgan. "Why is she here? Maybe she's betrothed to some brilliant European nobleman."

Morgan marveled at her smooth and graceful arms. Among the press of people, he watched her remove her long gloves with slender fingers, and his eyes drank in the sight of her. Morgan imagined himself to be a drab moth being drawn to the brightness of her flame. With wings beating, he was ready and willing to be burned.

What kind of man am I to allow myself these feelings? I know nothing about her, but I want to know everything. I doubt she'll even look in my direction.

All I can really see is her silhouette. She's slender, and seems taller than me.

I shouldn't be so easily dazzled. I need to get hold of myself. If I go up in flames, it's what I deserve.

Why am I drawn to her? It's almost against my will. If only Hetty will forgive this weakness I'm feeling....

Hetty's too good for me. I owe her my complete honesty.

I should tell her the problem, but I wouldn't know how. My funny sweet girl…it would hurt too much. But how can I live with myself if my thoughts are sneaky?

It would be wrong of me to seek out this woman. The only thing worse would be not to see her at all. I'll want to see her again and again, if she'll let me.

It's always been easy for me to talk to people, but what could I say to her?

She's looking over her shoulder toward me! Maybe she'll come this way.

Morgan held his breath as she approached. The soft silk of her blouse and the lines of her dress fell around the softness of her slender waist and glowed, as if with the joy of touching her.

Morgan forced his serious blue eyes away. Sheepishly, he looked at the floor like a small schoolboy.

He tried to focus on the glossy shoes of a nearby gentleman, but his eyes were soon drawn to her slim ankles. She wore a pair of satin high-heeled pumps with gleaming rhinestone buckles.

"I mustn't look," he thought, "or the vision of her will stay with me. When I'm with Hetty, will thoughts of her come between us? It would be wrong to always be thinking about what I've just seen…and to have this image in my mind."

The young woman turned her attention toward Morgan. The crowd separated. Faceless people in tuxedos and evening gowns rustled away, allowing him a long breathless moment to return her gaze.

She nodded gracefully to acknowledge him.

As she came closer, the bright lights behind her formed a halo of the braid encircling her head. Morgan's mouth went dry at the sight of her smooth and slender neck.

Why am I drawn to her? I need to get hold of myself.

His mind raced. "What should I say? I could tell her I'm marrying Hetty Lawrence, so don't get any closer. Stop being so beautiful.

"I can't bear the guilt. Don't make me explain my feelings to Hetty—and to myself."

He closed his eyes and spoke quietly to himself. "Oh, please don't touch me," he said. "I must stop wanting you to."

The woman came so close he could feel the warmth of her breath. The sweet scent of honeysuckle reached his nostrils. She said nothing, but stood silently before him.

Her hands reached out to touch his elbows lightly from beneath. Morgan's throat tightened with his rapid breathing. As his eyes drifted to her neck, the folds of her ruffled shawl fell away, and he saw the dimple in her chin.

It was Hetty's dimple.

In his confusion, Morgan felt the room spin. Was it a trick of the lights and cameras surrounding them? How *could* this be Hetty! Maybe he just wanted it to be. He lifted his eyes slowly.

Her smile was warm, but she looked at him quizzically.

"Morgan?" she whispered.

At that moment, Hetty's attendants gathered in full force and whisked her away officiously in accord with some previous plan.

Her sudden disappearance left Morgan panting with the rapture of disbelief and wonder. He must see Hetty again as soon as humanly possible!

After straining for another glimpse of her among the sea of heads, he finally found his seat and tried halfheartedly to converse with a bearded man across the table. The man's voice droned on and on like ocean waves heard through a conch shell, and Morgan struggled to keep his mind on the conversation.

The ecstasy of Morgan's emotional turmoil was most puzzling. He had always loved Hetty for her sweetness and purity. Had anything changed? He stirred restlessly, in guilty confusion.

He felt intoxicated with an unfamiliar excitement. Or was it joyous unrest?

Morgan glanced around the table until his eyes fell on the place card to the right of him. It said Hetty Lawrence!

As the crowd would not be settling down anytime soon, he excused himself to go for a brisk walk, hoping the cool outdoor air might calm the battle raging within him.

He must make sense of these unexpected feelings before seeing Hetty again.

CHAPTER ELEVEN

Her Hero

Outside the doors of the convention center, another drama was brewing. Early in the week, Ignatz had practiced his best lurking before the mirror until he passed his own high standards. He was now an excellent lurker. Eager to demonstrate his skills to Katrinka, he had come to town well before the appointed time and now hid in the shadows.

Ignatz knew the best policy was, *Always do unto others before they do unto you.* When training wild animals, he learned you can't leave safety to chance. He would have to apply that policy here, for sure. This Morganthal guy was quick.

Driven by pride in what he considered his superhuman abilities, Ignatz tried to blend in with his surroundings. It's not easy to think and act like a brick wall. Especially while fumbling with a bulky laundry bag and an assortment of handcuffs.

Ignatz glanced at his absolutely accurate torture-tested Timex watch. He had checked it earlier, just to be sure. Katrinka would be meeting him in exactly twenty-one minutes, to run through their plan one more time.

According to the long hand, it was almost dinnertime. Ignatz leaned against the wall. Maybe she would bring him a sandwich. His stomach was rumbling something awful. He tried to remember the smell of Katrinka's perfume, but mostly he thought how terrific some barbecued pork would smell.

Ignatz froze in place when he saw a man slowly turn the corner into the alley. What a lucky break! It was Morgan Morganthal, looking strangely confused. He would demonstrate to Katrinka that he was a man of action.

This would be a piece of cake. He'd have Morganthal tied up in the warehouse in short order and still get back in time to tell her about it.

The bag went over Morgan's head. "Gotcha!" said Ignatz. "Ha Ha!" In no time, he pulled the stunned captive in through a dark doorway off the alley. Morgan lay gagged and cuffed in an empty warehouse, with no idea what had happened.

It was a proud Ignatz who strutted back to the meeting place. "When that cupcake sees I already did it," he said, "I got it made in the shade."

Free Counsel and Advice

When Ignatz was in the appointed place, Katrinka was not. He'd have to find her later. Meanwhile, he returned to remove the sack covering his prisoner's head.

Morgan squinted and glanced around at the stark walls of the abandoned warehouse. His legs were bound to a solidly built metal chair, and his wrists were handcuffed behind him. Who was he dealing with? He waited quietly until a face appeared before him.

"Ignatz!" said Morgan. "Well, this is a surprise."

Ignatz cracked his knuckles. "Yeah." he said, raising one eyebrow the way he had rehearsed it. Like a man in control.

He kicked a scrap of lumber with authority and considered what to say next. Things were already going well, mostly because this cat wasn't going anywhere. Morgan's handcuffs inspired Ignatz with confidence. Small talk would be easy.

Morgan straightened his shoulders and asked, "So, Ignatz.... How's the family?"

"Family? What family?"

"Your family," said Morgan. "They're the reason I didn't want to fire you."

"Oh, that family! I wasn't sure what you meant."

Morgan sat back so the handcuffs wouldn't dig into his wrists. "You told me about your sick little boy. You do have a son, don't you?"

"Well, yes. Yes, of course. But I mean, I don't have him yet."

"Yet?" said Morgan.

"Well, I was inferring about the family I'm *going* to have. A guy's got to take 'sponsibility, you know."

"Of course. And your wife?" Morgan asked gently.

"Yes. Thank you for asking."

"You do have one, don't you?"

Ignatz forgot to raise his eyebrow. "Well," he said, "why do you want to know? That's a real interpersonal question, and I ought to have a attorney on my person before I answer it."

"Actually," said Morgan, "I'm a lawyer, you know, so feel free to explain, although it's a bit challenging to take notes with these handcuffs on."

That gave Ignatz something to think about, but he didn't appear to know what it was.

Morgan began again. "What seems to be the issue here, Ignatz?"

"The issue is that I'm in charge here, because I've had

enough of not being, you know, in charge. Nobody respects me, and it ain't right. I'm a perfectly respectacle human being, and I deserve as much indignity as the next guy. It wasn't right I got sacked. I was just doing my job.

"And another thing, if you'd been me, you wouldn't have got plummeted by that elephant."

"How's that?" asked Morgan.

"I'd show it who's boss."

Morgan glared at him. "I know," he said. "I've seen how you do it."

Ignatz kicked at a crack in the cement floor. "You don't understand," he said. "Stupid animals. They don't have a brain. People…'specially dames…they get real 'motional. Like as if animals had feelings and stuff. All elephants know is they won't do it no more if it hurts."

"But you say they don't have feelings," said Morgan.

"Well, not as such, so to speak, if you know what I mean."

Morgan's deep blue eyes were fixed on Ignatz. "Not really," he said. "Did you learn that from Blossom, after you saw a certain amount of blood?"

"Well, I learned a lot from this cool cat from Eastern Europe. When I met the guy, I knew I wanted to be him."

"His name wasn't Ignatz, was it?"

"Well, why'd you think that?" There was a long pause before Ignatz began again.

"I mean, yeah, that's the name my mother should have gave me."

"I know," said Morgan. "It's not our fault what name we get."

Ignatz cracked his knuckles in agreement. "Yeah! We're a baby, for crying out loud, so how come they do that to us? Ignatz. That's my real name."

"I didn't say it's not."

Ignatz froze in place. "You know," he said. "I can tell

you know."

"The way I see it," said Morgan, "Ignatz is your name. You can't help what's on the records."

"You seen records? Like law kind of stuff?"

"Your records are safe with me," said Morgan. "Why tell anyone else? It's not their business."

"I don't get it," said Ignatz. "You knew and you didn't blab it all over?"

"Well, we wouldn't want the word to get out and damage your reputation. Especially with that sick little boy you don't have yet."

"Yeah, that's right. And my wife, too."

Morgan nodded. "But she won't care so much what your first name is," he said. "She'll mostly want to have your *last* name."

Ignatz brightened. "You think? Thanks, Mr. Morganthal!" He took a moment to chew absently on a fingernail before he continued. "She's not exactly free to hitch up with me right now," he said, "but when she is, I sure won't be telling her my real name."

"That doesn't sound too promising, Ignatz. Once she finds out, will she ever trust you again?"

"Well, she's got this handsome, rich husband, but we're real solid anyways."

"I see," said Morgan. "And she won't fancy someone else after she marries you?"

"Huh?"

"I'm just saying, Ignatz…that's not what I'd want."

"Ha! That's what you think!" He dropped his keys and picked them up again. "Like I say, it's me she fancies."

Actually, what Ignatz fancied most, at the moment, was a thick burger dripping with cheese and onions, and a chocolate milkshake with a fat straw.

A Change of Heart

Katrinka and Tilly got to the convention hall a little late in the evening and rushed to their hotel room. There they quickly placed their bags on the beds, and to be helpful, Tilly hung Katrinka's wedding dress on the back of the door. They hurried to the banquet hall.

Katrinka was to lure Morgan outside, but it was already past the appointed time. She anxiously sought an opportunity to slip away unnoticed. Ignatz would be waiting. How could she possibly explain to him that suddenly this whole kidnapping business seemed wrong? She had changed her plans, and he would want to know why.

There were many reasons. While they were working together on the funeral, Morgan had been gentle with her tender feelings, and he made sure everything happened just as she wanted.

Without his steady guidance, she could never have blundered her way through the process. Her tears and the many memories they shared seemed to touch Morgan.

Katrinka found her mind straying to events of the past week.

Daddy couldn't make Morgan love me while he was alive, but he's making it happen now, with his death.

Things are going my way. Morgan will choose me. I feel sure of him now. I won't have to trick him into going outside or lure him into a trap. All I have to do is pay off Ignatz when I get there.

The whole plan was ridiculous anyway. I know Daddy wouldn't approve. I couldn't find Morgan at the banquet, so maybe that could be my excuse.

By now Morgan can see how well suited I am to be his wife, and how perfect we are together.

Joseph says maybe I should try to look plain like Hetty. I suppose that way I could beat her at her own game.

Last week, when I asked if I should wear my eyelashes, Morgan laughed and said, "Not unless you're afraid of catching cold." I guess that meant he didn't have an opinion.

Whether I wear my eyelashes or not, we'll be a gorgeous couple. Tilly knows I've brought my wedding dress with me, so she's expecting big news. She can help get the public on my side.

Joseph says I should try to act interested in the things Morgan is doing, the way Hetty does. Whatever it takes.

I think Daddy's death is almost as hard for Morgan as it is for me. If I'd cared more about the circus all these years, I'd have more to talk about with Morgan.

It won't hurt to get acquainted with Hetty like Daddy wanted. If Morgan sees us together, the contrast will show him how awkward she is.

Tilly appeared slightly annoyed at her companion's lack of attention. When Katrinka read her expression, she spoke the first words that came to her mind.

"Morgan says lions aren't as unpredictable as elephants," she said.

This comment in no way answered the question Tilly had just asked concerning the length of hemlines.

"But," said Katrinka, "according to P.T. Barnum, when entertaining the public, it's best to have an elephant." She flashed her dimples and looked around for Morgan.

Katrinka thought of something else that did not concern hemlines. "Morgan says I should see *The Big Circus*, if it's still in the theaters. They used a real famous trapeze artist as a consultant," she said. "In case you ever heard of Barbette. The name didn't mean anything to me, but Victor Mature and Rhonda Fleming are in it. Want to go?"

Katrinka knew Morgan would be impressed if she seemed to have some interest in it, so she was glad Tilly agreed to accompany her.

"But won't Morgan want to see it with you?" asked Tilly.

"Oh, of course!" said Katrinka, "He never wants to leave my side. But we're together so constantly, it will do him good to pine after me once in a while." She sighed, and pressing a hand against her chest, she felt through the fabric of her blouse for the diamond ring.

Katrinka took satisfaction in the hope that, by candlelight, she would still be lovely without her Fanatalash brand eyelashes. Certainly her hair was just as stunning as ever.

Once again she fell into deep thought, this time about personal fame and glory.

I really ought to be in the movies. Daddy would have taken everybody he knows to a movie, if I was a star.

Morgan must know a beautiful woman can open doors. Hetty's nothing but a tall scarecrow. She'd have people slamming doors in his face.

I want to remember all the things Daddy used to say. He thinks I ought to associate with people who are good. He must have meant people like Morgan.

But he thinks I should listen to what Joseph says, too.

Daddy thought I might learn something from Hetty if she became a friend. I really don't know what it might be.

After developing the courage to send Ignatz away, Katrinka was anxious to do so. It was impossible for her to sit still even a minute longer. "Will you excuse me, Tilly dear?" she said. "I'll be right back."

Tilly watched Katrinka sashay a short distance across the banquet hall, until suddenly a tall, elegant young woman approached, apparently taking her completely by surprise. They stood together and spoke a moment, searching for someone as they talked. An instant later they parted, vanishing into the crowd.

Wrinkle Phobia

Katrinka stepped into the bathroom of her hotel room and stood before the mirror. Why did Hetty Lawrence have to be here! The sight of her had been a shock.

Still shaken by the girl's appearance, Katrinka's hands quivered with emotion while wiping the tears from her cheeks.

Before long, Hetty would meet her here in the room. Katrinka breathed deeply and wondered if she had the strength to remain calm. There were some little lines at the corners of her eyes that she hadn't seen before.

She longed to hear her father's soothing voice.

Daddy, what should I do? Everything's different now because of Hetty. I wonder what could have happened to make her look pretty. I've got to keep Morgan from seeing her.

You wanted me to make friends with her. Maybe that can be my excuse for keeping her here, out of sight.

Now I need Ignatz for sure. We'll have to go through with the kidnapping. I have no choice. When it's absolutely necessary, it's not wrong, is it?

I refuse to feel guilty about it, because I'm doing it for you, Daddy.

You said family is everything, so if I make Morgan part of our family in the end, won't that make everything all right?

I wish I could remember more of what you said. You were everything to me. Hetty's the one who's changed the rules of the game.

When Morgan and I are married, I don't want children.

Maybe deep down, I only want them if they look like you. But what if they aren't as good at being dwarfs as you? How can I be a good mother without your help?

I'm so mixed up.

Did you like how we honored you, Daddy?

Katrinka lay down on the bed and cried softly until she was able to gain control of her emotions.

Concerned she might be making more wrinkles, Katrinka forced herself to sit on the corner of the bed. She tilted her chin upward at a confident angle.

You were right, Daddy. Morgan will always love the circus. He's talking about being a partner with Max like you were. He was excited to tell me, and I tried real hard to act interested.

It was like we were children again. He even smiled at me like he cares. We talked about the time we made mud cakes and decorated them with colored pebbles and sang happy birthday to the seagulls.

He could have asked me to give back the diamond, but he didn't.

I wasn't frightened riding on the elephant. Not with Morgan near me. The strength in his face gave me confidence. It was like a sign that together we can control the business.

Just because Hetty Lawrence had some sort of hocus-pocus happen to her, she's still a complete nobody. Too tall and shapeless to find a husband.

I feel kind of sorry for her. She's colorless and stupid. Completely out of her league and definitely not Morgan's type. She should go to law school and share an office with her papa. He could use a little help blowing his nose.

Morgan won't need to practice law or bother with the bar exam. There won't be time for that kind of nonsense. I'll make him move out of the law office after we're married.

He still wants to fly, and I said I'd go up in the glider with

Morgan will call me his beloved little sweetie.

him. He seemed really surprised. Of course I won't do anything of the sort when we're married. But for now I'll say whatever I must. I want Morgan too much to give up.

I adore his handsome face. The way he looks when the light falls a certain way over his cheeks, the angle of his jaw is strong and manly, and I can see he is perfect for me. When he walks into a room people can tell he's important. His powerful body makes everyone sit up and notice.

When he smiles, I always watch his lips to see if they might invite me to kiss him, but they never do. I could go mad just listening to the sound of his voice.

Do you think he'll notice my wrinkles?

He'll be your son-in-law soon, Daddy. I promise. It will be my gift to you.

We'll have all the money we could ever want, and I'll have a different mink coat for every day of the week.

For our first anniversary, I'll make him buy me a pink silk negligee with Belgian lace. He'll get the servants to bring me breakfast in bed, and I'll order fresh poached figs and little puff pastries with creamed eggs. Once a week, a girl wearing a starched uniform will give me a manicure in my own dressing room.

Morgan will call me his beloved little sweetie and worship the ground I walk on. Partly because of how good we look together, but mainly because his father will make him filthy rich if he marries me.

Oh, Daddy, we're going to be so happy!

There was a tentative knock on the door. Katrinka chose to keep Hetty waiting briefly while she checked the little lines by her eyes once more. When she had refreshed her make-up, the mirror told her she was more than ready to take command.

As she faced the door, Katrinka decided not to have her wedding dress visible. She put it back in its box and slid it under the bed rather than appear too sure of herself.

CHAPTER TWELVE

Closer Than Ever

While Hetty waited outside Katrinka's hotel room, she tried to organize her thoughts. All that came to her mind were the words of the poem, *Come into my parlor, said the spider to the fly.*

"It's like I'm going into Katrinka's web," she thought, "and she's about to devour me. But I should keep in mind how much she needs friends, especially now."

Katrinka slid the bolt, removed the chain, and opened the door a crack. "Oh, there you are!" she said.

"I'm sorry," said Hetty. "I meant to come straight up, but I took a wrong turn."

Katrinka widened the crack in the door. "Weren't you going to your school reunion? I was surprised to see you here."

"Yes," said Hetty. "I mean no, I was too."

"Let me guess. You got lost," said Katrinka. "You often have a certain lost look about you."

Hetty twisted her handkerchief. "I do? I guess maybe

so…. I'm with a group of generous people though," said Hetty. "The Di Milanos. They helped me when my bags were stolen."

"Di Milanos?" said Katrinka. "I know them. Sabrina models for Di Milano."

"We made an arrangement," said Hetty. "I replaced Sabrina. And in exchange, they replaced a lot of what was taken."

Katrinka smiled and opened the door to admit Hetty. "I see they went a little overboard," she said. "What an absolute nightmare, you poor dear! Really though, you must be happy for a toothbrush and a change of clothes."

Katrinka's luscious pink lips drew back in a dimpled smile. "Don't be too hard on them," she said, "just because you look ridiculous. I'm sure they mean well, bless their hearts."

Hetty tried not to twist her handkerchief. "Yes," she said. "They have big hearts." Katrinka's display of confidence somehow did nothing to increase her own.

Katrinka removed her pink suitcase from a little footstool. "Please sit here," she said, "and tell me about it."

Hetty took a gasping breath. "About the funeral procession. It was a moving experience for everyone. If the burial was anything like the procession," she said, "I know it must have been beautiful, too."

Katrinka tilted her head wistfully. "It was," she said. "Morgan was magnificent." Her moist eyes gazed dreamily into space. "I could never have suffered through it without his shoulder to cry on.

"He was involved in all the details," said Katrinka, "to make sure it was in good taste. We weren't aware of anything like it being done before, and Morgan worried about whether it might offend anyone."

Hetty nodded. She looked down at her twisted handkerchief and wondered, had Katrinka really cried with her head on Morgan's shoulder? Maybe it was just an expression.

A sweet little sigh came from Katrinka's lips, and she continued. "Morgan and I go way back, you know. We laughed about the time I kissed him when he was six years old and I was nine."

Hetty felt the color drain from her face. She thought, "Could anything like that have happened more recently? With Phil gone, I'm sure she needs Morgan more than ever."

"I was wondering," said Katrinka, "has Morgan seen you? I mean have you seen each other yet?"

Hetty gripped her knees, hoping to control the trembling of her hands. "Not really," she said. "Well, just briefly. The Di Milanos needed me, then Morgan left right after I saw him. I just assumed he would take his place at the table after that."

"So he saw you?"

"Yes," said Hetty, "and I'm worried that he was upset about what he saw."

"Does that matter?" Katrinka blinked languidly. "Men know nothing about fashion and makeup."

"I think maybe he's avoiding me," said Hetty.

"Yes, but we can't worry about what other people think, can we?" said Katrinka. "We need to be ourself. Looking beautiful doesn't change who you are inside. Any man who thinks it does must be awfully wishy-washy in his affection. His feelings must not run very deep."

Hetty tried to look directly into Katrinka's face, but had to avert her eyes.

Katrinka began again. "If he doesn't appreciate your efforts to look your best, the relationship was far too fragile to begin with. You can't count on men," she said with assurance.

Hetty thought it best to change the topic. "The way your father loved you," she said, "it was a beautiful thing.

And it didn't have anything to do with your appearance."

"Are you sure?"

"I'm sure," said Hetty. "He said you were kind and thoughtful in many ways. Also that you don't need to rely on your looks as much as you do."

Katrinka's eyes widened. "Did he say all that to your face?"

"Yes, to my face," said Hetty, "and I believe it. If you are your best self, the way your father sees you inside, it couldn't possibly make you less beautiful. Also," she said, "he wanted us to be friends."

Katrinka leaned closer. For a time she appeared too puzzled to speak.

Then she raised her chin as if to assert her obvious position of superiority and said, "By the bye, Morgan considers you such a nice acquaintance, you being his sister Melinda's friend, and so on. Feel free to write him a note of sympathy.

"As busy as Morgan is, I rather imagine he will read it. Especially if I deliver it and tell him to. Daddy's death has been hard for Morgan, too, you know. It's a bond we will always have."

Katrinka smiled sweetly and continued. "We're closer now than ever."

Hetty felt the desperation of being trapped in her web.

Guts and Values

Ignatz couldn't remember where he got the handcuffs. Morgan had asked if they came from a Cracker Jack box. Ignatz said it wasn't his fault if they dug into his wrists. Besides, all the others he brought were the same.

"Ignatz," said Morgan, "what kind of child were you?"

"Well, let's just say I was real recessive about everything back then."

"Recessive?" asked Morgan.

"Yeah. You know, when everything's got to be perfect or you go nuts?"

Morgan nodded. "Right," he said.

"I was a real smart punk, as you might inflect. But you know how it is. My teachers allowed as how I might learn best from experience. They were right, some of us don't need school to make us smart."

Ignatz thought with pride of how he'd read every one of his comic books and movie magazines. Even the big words. It was a lot of work, but you don't get ahead without reading. "Rich as Morganthal is," he thought, "I'll bet he doesn't have as many comic books as me."

He knew Morgan could use a little advice. "It's all a matter of guts," said Ignatz. "You got to have guts to make it in life. Guts and values."

Ignatz thought of how much progress he'd made since the day he stormed out of junior high school.

The history teacher wanted me to write three pages about some king. The guy was dead, for crying out loud! Garbage like that was a genuine waste of time.

Actually, the guy didn't even get to be king in the end. Scads of people wanted him for king, but he settled for having his face on the one-dollar bill instead. A puny one-dollar bill! That's when I walked out and never returned.

That took guts.

Morgan seemed increasingly interested. He said, "Tell me about your values, Ignatz."

"I'm a collector, see," said Ignatz. "I buy stuff when the guy says it's a good value. I got me lots of values. You got to use your smarts, though. That's what good collectors do."

Ignatz stopped and frowned. "Hey, I got to go get me a burger. You'll still be here when I get back."

"I'm not promising anything," said Morgan.

"What, you saying I didn't tie you up good?"

Morgan shifted his weight. "Whoever put you up to this," he said, "that's who should bring you a hamburger."

"You think?" asked Ignatz.

"Sure. It's no easy matter, kidnapping people," said Morgan. "Food ought to be one of the perks. You can't be expected to take the risk without better working conditions."

"Yeah. What if you hadn't been such a pushover?"

"What are they paying you?" asked Morgan.

"That's between me and uh…me and them."

"If I were you, Ignatz, I'd call them. Just put the phone to your stomach. When they hear it, they'll get the picture."

Ignatz glanced at the payphone behind Morgan and explored one pocket at a time. Somewhere he had the phone number of Katrinka's hotel. But maybe he shouldn't call just yet.

Morgan's dark blue eyes showed sympathy for his plight, and Ignatz returned to the subject of his impressive remarkableness. "They use to call me incorrigible," he said, "but know what? I showed them. What I did was I got corrigible." He raised his chin a notch. "And I did it all on my own."

"How's that?"

"I learned you gotta be serene and comatose," he said brightly.

"Comatose?" asked Morgan.

"Yeah. You know, calm. Relaxed. That way you can always be irrational under pressure."

Morgan glanced briefly at the rattrap next to the wall of the warehouse. "I'd appreciate it if I could go back to my dinner," said Morgan. "I need to meet someone."

It was not clear to Ignatz how to proceed, but he flared his nostrils as if to say, "Why should you get the grub, and not me?"

"Tell you what," said Ignatz. "I might call your honey. Maybe she'll think you're worth a few bucks. Or she could get me a burger."

"What makes you think she's in town?" said Morgan.

"I *know* she is," said Ignatz, tapping his skull.

He followed that with a useful trick he learned in the movies: *When in doubt, act mysterious.* Ignatz was confident the rumble in his stomach did not destroy the desired air of mystery.

Morgan's expression grew somber. He fell silent and appeared to be deep in thought.

Tangled Threads

At the Morganthal estate, the evening meal was over. Max and Mimi both arose and moved toward the window, standing a slight distance apart. Melinda remained at the table, watching the private and subtle looks that passed between her parents. At first they appeared to be watching the moon over the darkened gatehouse.

Mimi was the first to speak. "Phil can't be far away, Max," she said. "Not when you feel as if he's so near."

He smiled at her words of comfort. "But you," he said, "... you're the one who's near."

They remained silent and appeared comfortable with no words between them.

Melinda leaned forward, preparing to leave, but must have thought better of it.

The warmth of this quiet moment remained undisturbed.

Her eyes wandered to the buffet. Each night after dinner, the drinks had come out of hiding to rest there on the silver tray. After dinner, after lunch, or any other occasion. The decanter and the crystal goblets were not there tonight. And no bottles were visible through the glass panes of the cabinet door.

Melinda looked again at her mother. Mimi's skirt brushed against the drapery. Her fingers played with the gold silk tassel. "Max," she said, "Morgan is more like you than I ever knew." She tangled the threads and then stroked them rather absently for a time, apparently with continued thoughts of Morgan.

The threads were soft and unruly as the down of a dandelion.

When Mimi had finished taming the silken threads, she turned to Max and spoke. "She's exactly right for him," she said. Her thought was presented as a final proclamation.

Max stared across the sculpture gardens at the darkened windows of the gatehouse. He was puzzled. "Do you mean it?" he said.

"She shares his dreams," said Mimi, "She'll know his heart the way she knows mine."

Mimi turned her eyes toward the moon and recited Shakespeare's words:

> *"He is the half part of a blessed man,*
> *Left to be finished by such as she;*
> *And she a fair divided excellence,*
> *Whose fullness of perfection lies in him."*

Melinda left quietly, looking somewhat puzzled. Her departure went unnoticed.

When Pigs Fly

In her hotel room, Katrinka was making great progress against Hetty. She had even been able to pose herself where the reading lamp would conceal the little wrinkles around her eyes. Hetty was sure to withdraw from this competition.

"That's what it is," thought Katrinka. "A competition for Morgan. A contest of will and beauty."

She drew back her glossy pink lips in her most coy smile and tilted her head toward Hetty, once again demonstrating her dominance. "Hetty Lawrence," she thought, "you'll win when pigs fly!"

The phone rang on the other side of the bed, and Katrinka excused herself with an officious air. "I apologize, Hetty dear. This could be important, but do make yourself comfortable," she said. "Yes, hello?" She cupped her hand over the receiver as if wishing privacy. It was Ignatz.

"They gave me a real hard time," he said. "I asked for Karrinka Morganthal, and they said there couldn't be any such person as you to whom I wished to speak to, but now I got you. And guess what. I also got me one Morgan Morganthal! Who knows what might happen…. It's looking real dangerous for him here, like I say. But it'll be a whole bunch less dangerous when you've brung me a burger."

Katrinka could hear Morgan's voice. "Katrinka?" he asked. He sounded puzzled.

"See?" said Ignatz. He was apparently speaking to Morgan. "Like I told you. Your honey, she's in town, all right. She's come for these beauty meetings, and you didn't even know it! Ha! Now ask her for cash."

"Sorry, I can't do that, Ignatz."

"What, you looking to have a real short life, or what?" said

Ignatz. "I'll hold the phone so I can hear what you're saying."

"You can hear me anyway. I'm sitting next to you," said Morgan. "In handcuffs, I remind you."

"Well, if your wife knows what's good for you, she'll do as I say."

"My what?" said Morgan.

Katrinka waited to hear Morgan's voice again, but all she could hear was Ignatz saying, "Go on, sir. Tell her you're scared."

She heard Morgan clear his throat. "I can't tell her anything," he said. "You're holding the phone upside down."

Katrinka waited a moment then staged a resonant response. "Oh, you're so brave, sweetheart!" She stretched herself dramatically across the bed. "You know I'll do anything for you, Morgan dearest." Her discreet whispers were designed to make Hetty feel like an intruder. "I'll never leave you again, I promise," she said.

Morgan sounded even more confused. "Katrinka, what on earth are you saying?"

"I love you, too," she said.

There was muffled talking, then Morgan's puzzled voice again. "I don't think I'm hearing you correctly," he said. There was a brief pause. "Did you come with Tilly Teller?"

"Yes," said Katrinka, "and I'll never let her come between us again, I promise."

"Ask for cash," yelled Ignatz.

Morgan spoke up. "I think Ignatz could use a big hamburger," he said. "Could you manage that? Together with a milkshake?"

"Oh, yes!" crooned Katrinka. "Together, darling. Always together, I promise." She languidly fanned the air with her eyelashes.

There was more muffled talking, then she heard Morgan ask, "Did you want chocolate? Ignatz, hold the phone to my mouth so I can tell her."

Ignatz spoke into the phone next. "Yeah, chocolate," he said, "A big one. I'll meet you by the lift. West of the warehouse ramp."

"And I'm just as eager to see you," said Katrinka breathlessly.

Then came the muffled voice of Ignatz. "Ain't she a doozie!" he said.

Katrinka sensed a soft rustling nearby. Hetty had risen to leave. Soon the door closed quietly, and Katrinka found herself alone.

Smiling, she spoke again into the phone. "I'll be there in a minute," she said then slowly hung up the receiver. "Hetty will learn pigs don't fly," she said to herself.

Before leaving to meet Ignatz, Katrinka looked in the bathroom mirror. She had to think things out.

Hetty says if I were like Daddy sees me, I'd still be beautiful. It's hard to respect someone who's so naïve that she's even nice to me.

I'm sure Hetty's not very observant. But if I let the name Ignatz slip, she'll catch on and call the police.

Maybe she didn't notice my wrinkles.

Oh no! They look worse than before. Especially on the left. Maybe egg whites would fix them. Or cucumber slices might tighten them up.

Oh, Daddy! This isn't some kind of warning, is it? What have I done? Am I being punished? I just know I'm being punished!

But I didn't lie to Hetty. Not really. I was only acting.

CHAPTER THIRTEEN

Fire in her Eyes

Ignatz leaned against the cinderblock wall and positioned himself directly under the bare light bulb. He waited and thought through his big dream.

She'll flip when she sees me looking so good.

I used a actual comb. And I brushed my teeth with Ipana. A guy's got to dream big to get ahead in this world!

Right off, I'll say, "My, my." I'll say it real casual, like as if I was Tony Curtis. She'll be speechless at first, so then I'll say, "Cat got your tongue?"

I'll say clever stuff like that. She'll inedibly be impressed.

While he waited, Ignatz raised one eyebrow and flexed the tattoo on his arm just for practice.

When Katrinka came around the corner, all his well-rehearsed words left him at the sight of her.

"Oh, Ignatz!" she purred. "You were simply magnificent!"

"You think?" He puffed out his chest. In a voice deep

as humanly possible, he said, "I was doing my bery vest, Ladyship. I mean.…That is, I only done what comes natural."

Ignatz waited for her to throw herself into his arms, declaring him to be the handsome hero of her dreams, but Katrinka merely handed over the greasy sack containing the hamburger and milkshake.

He couldn't smell the burger, but her perfume made his head spin.

Her little white teeth gleamed under the light bulb. "I brought fries too," she said. A large moth, flitting around the light bulb, cast an eerie shadow around them.

Katrinka reached her hand into her purse. "That will be all," she said, "and here's your ticket home."

"Huh? That's it?" said Ignatz.

"For now, anyway," she said. "I'll take over from here." Anxious to see Morgan, she looked eagerly at the warehouse entrance.

Ignatz shifted his weight uneasily. "I thought maybe it was more like, you know, otherwise," he said. "Me and you, that is."

Katrinka put her hands on her hips. "Dear sweet Ignatz," she said, "you've misunderstood me, I'm afraid."

This was a bad turn of events, but Ignatz was not one to give up. "This Morganthal," he said, "He's not a bad guy. Just not much of a husband, is he?' He winked. "Now if it was me, I'd do right by you."

She glanced at the entrance again. "You think you could hold a candle to him?" she said.

"Hey, look here," said Ignatz. "What kind of guy you think I am, anyways? I wouldn't do nothing like that. Besides, it's not him what got me sacked, on account of.… Well, he just didn't. Bet it was that idiot midget who runs things."

In the light of the bulb, Ignatz suddenly saw fire in Katrinka's eyes. Confused, he stepped back. "Hey," he said,

"What'd I do wrong? You going to give me a knuckle sandwich?"

She shook with rage. "Don't you dare talk about my father that way," she said. "It's you who's the idiot! You bungled it. You were supposed to wait for me to bring Morgan out."

"Man!" he said, "you're cute all cranked up like this."

She glared at him. "Do you think I'd be doing this, if Morgan was really my husband?" she said.

There was a long, uneasy pause.

"He ain't your husband?" said Ignatz. He looked around to make sure there were no witnesses to his humiliation. He narrowed his eyes. "Don't rattle your cage, lady," he hissed. "And don't you dare fake a mool out of me."

Katrinka stared at Ignatz as if piecing together what had happened. In no time at all she appeared to have the answer.

"You wanted to work for the circus," she said, "but you didn't have enough experience. You just pretended to know animals. That's the real reason you got fired," she said. "You figured if you wanted something, you would lie to get it."

In rage, Ignatz moved closer. "And you lied to me 'cause you wanted something," he said. "It was your little joke, and I ain't laughing," he said.

He grabbed Katrinka by both wrists. "It's my joke, now," he said. The sack dropped, and his milkshake burst on the asphalt.

Ignatz jerked both her arms behind her back and tied them roughly with coarse rope. The heel of her shoe collapsed with the weakness in her knees, and Katrinka stumbled into the chocolate liquid, scraping her knee.

"Now for the cash," he said. "Get it or be wasted."

"But I don't have any money. I don't, Ignatz!" Her lip trembled.

"Who cares," he said. "You got a rich boyfriend."

"Not really," she said, crying softly. "I'll find a way. Don't tell him."

Katrinka tried to wipe her hands on the asphalt, which added dirt to the stickiness of the chocolate milkshake. Ignatz sneered and pulled her to a standing position. "Like how?" he asked.

Her voice was weak. "Well," she said, "he gets the money if he marries me."

"No lie?"

Fat City

With Katrinka now securely fastened to a chair in the warehouse, Ignatz went to his hotel room for a quick break. He needed to think.

Leaning his neck against the back of the couch, he hit his head on the wall. "How 'noying," he mumbled. He scowled to show a general irritation with his hotel room, the TV set, and whatever else crossed his mind.

An oily hamburger wrapper lay beside him on the couch. Crumpling it into a ball, he lobbed it unsuccessfully at the TV screen.

"News, news, news," he muttered. "What do I care?"

He had bigger ideas. To keep his mind alert, he reviewed one of them now.

I hate how everything's got invented already. They should have invented one more thing. A long pole or whatnot for flipping channels from a ways off.

Just 'cause they didn't, I gotta move my wazoo off this couch. I hate hearing about baloney what don't matter, like government.

Leastways, I got Morganthal and that dolly tied up. They're

I hate how everything's got invented already.

too far apart to jabber and cook anything up.

Maybe they think my brain is interior to theirs. Ha! I got it all worked out.

I get them married. That makes them rich. I get their cash. Simple as that.

Of course I gotta work out the intrinsic details. Like how do I do it without they run away and squeal on me?

Ignatz continued his brooding until right after the Jergens lotion ad. Then the TV reporter turned his attention to the beauty convention. He repeated news and interviews from earlier in the day.

Raising one eyebrow, Ignatz listened with interest. He figured a guy like him who was holding two beauty people captive could consider himself practically an expert on stuff like this.

The announcer was wandering the halls of the convention center, searching for news relating to the fashion industry. In the course of it, he started a conversation with a man whose face was familiar to Ignatz.

"If I may, Mr. Morganthal," said the reporter.

Ignatz perked right up. It was his Morganthal! He even wore the same red tie on TV. The very same one he had on tonight, in real life.

As the crowd jostled them, the man explained Morgan's stature and importance within the industry. Then he said, "Mr. Morganthal, you know the stars of the business world. Please tell our listeners, in your opinion, who are some of those men? I hope to interview them, this evening.... The movers and shakers, so to speak."

"I'm glad you asked," said Morgan. "Some of the finest designers and executives behind the scenes are women. It's also true in the businesses with which I'm more familiar. Circus management, insurance, shipping, and so on. Women who set the trends often go unrecognized. Let's get them out front."

"I can understand your bias," said the reporter, "because of your engagement to Katrinka Wallace. Miss Wallace is employed by your own company, I do believe?" His sly expression seemed to say, "Nya nya, I trapped you."

He continued. "Tell us about that, Mr. Morganthal. Our audience is quite familiar with the beauty queen, Miss Wallace."

"I'd be glad to," said Morgan. "Miss Wallace and I have been acquainted for many years. I'm confident she'll make a name for herself in fashion circles. As for my personal plans," he said, "I'm committed to someone else."

"Oh...my apologies!" said the embarrassed reporter.

Morgan smiled. "That's all right," he said, "It's a perfectly understandable mistake."

The announcer appeared relieved. He fumbled noisily with his papers. "Oh!" he said. "In fact I do have it right here in my notes. Her name is Henrietta Lawrence, I believe? Sorry, Mr. Morganthal! I thought it was a typo."

Ignatz could hardly believe his good fortune. He flexed the dancing girl on his bicep and smiled. For once he'd learned something useful in the news. "Henrietta Lawrence!" he said. "She'll be my ticket to Fat City!" Flaring his nostrils over his certain triumph, Ignatz leapt from the couch.

A Dead Cat

That same night, Marian Locke also found a good use for cheeseburgers. She picked up three of them at a fast food restaurant. Her brother Joseph would be coming to supper, and the tuna fish casserole she made had caught on fire.

Not just the crumbled potato chips on top; the whole thing tasted smoky.

Leaf would probably tell her it was a pleasant reminder of meals eaten when fighting forest fires or something of the sort, but she knew Joseph would push it around on his plate for long intervals between sips of water.

While Joseph was finishing a second wedge of the apple pie Leaf had made, Marian said, "Would you mind a little sisterly advice, Joseph?"

Joseph glanced at Leaf and grinned. "You see? This is why Dad told me to find my sister."

Marian put on a serious face so Joseph wouldn't take her words lightly, in his usual good-natured way.

"About Katrinka," she said. "I want you to have a realistic picture of life with her. It might not be what you're hoping for." Marian continued with more animation. "She always has to be the main attraction," she said. "She's sort of like Teddy Roosevelt. They say he was *'the bride at every wedding and the corpse at every funeral.'*"

Joseph's eyes conveyed his amusement. "And the centerpiece at every table," he said. "That's my Katrinka, all right, and it suits me fine. I like to sit back and watch."

"Another thing," said Marian, "maybe she'll never get over Morgan. Or her father. She practically worshipped Phil, you know."

His eyes twinkled. "So, what are you saying…she has good taste?"

Marian wasn't through. "I'm honestly not concerned about her standards," she said. "Or her basic morality."

She began again. "But marriage is hard enough as it is.

"It's not easy living with someone like me. I didn't know how much help I'd need from Leaf, just to grow up."

Leaf fidgeted with his napkin. The girl he married was a

constant surprise. He blushed at her frankness and reached for her hand under the table.

"Anyway," she said, "There could be worse things than a flirtatious wife, but think about it, Joseph. You and Katrinka aren't a likely match.

"Why not?" he asked.

"Well, once upon a time you were interested in Hetty. Those two are complete opposites."

"Right." He grinned.

"So you can see that, Joseph?"

Hooking both thumbs in his belt loops, he tipped back in his chair. "Absolutely," he said. "Hetty's unavailable, and Katrinka's not."

"True enough," said Marian. She took a big breath.

"It's just that for my brother, I might be less unenthusiastic if she weren't so openly not unavailable."

"Hold on!" Joseph threw back his head and laughed.

"Let me restate that," said Marian. "You can't swing a dead cat without hitting one of her ex-boyfriends."

A Nose for News

Tilly Teller hadn't traveled all the way to this convention merely to twiddle her thumbs and wait for a plate of food. When Katrinka excused herself from the banquet and walked away, that was all the excuse Tilly was looking for. If she could find Morgan Morganthal, maybe he would grant her an interview.

Even after a thorough search, Tilly found no sign of either of them. Wherever Katrinka had gone, very likely Morgan was a part of the story.

Tilly could boast she was born with a nose for news,

and she followed that nose straight back to her hometown.

Max Morganthal was sure to provide some spellbinding answers to intrigue the faithful readers of her *Tilly Tells All* column. When she called ahead, he proved surprisingly willing to hold a late meeting with her.

After resting briefly on the train, Tilly arrived looking refreshed and excited. She took a taxi directly to the Morganthal estate, arriving later that same night.

A servant guided Tilly through a maze of rooms to meet with Max. They found him seated in a large leather armchair, wearing a green satin lounging jacket. He was reading aloud to his wife from *The Complete Works of Shakespeare*.

Mimi sat on the ottoman rubbing his ankles, but excused herself with a start. Max stood, offered Tilly a chair and put on his slippers.

After hearing her report, Max frowned and said, "This makes no sense. There are too many people Morgan was supposed to meet."

"I looked everywhere," said Tilly, "and asked everyone who should know."

"People don't just go 'poof' like that," said Max. "Mimi!" he called. "It's about Morgan and Katrinka.... Sounds like they weren't at the convention."

Mimi looked in through the door but had nothing to say.

Tilly leaned forward and opened her mouth. She didn't wait for them to ask her opinion. "I think they've eloped," she said.

"No. They have not eloped," said Mimi.

"My wife is right," said Max.

Tilly glanced from one to the other. "Tell me then," she said, "why is her wedding dress missing? I hung it on the hotel door, and now it's gone."

No one had an answer.

Suddenly Tilly's eyes darted around the room. "Let me think," she said. "I believe she might have mentioned where they were going on their honeymoon. Some place called Ignatz...

"Yes, that's it. I think they were going to Ignatz.... I'm not familiar with the place," she said.

Max scowled. "Ignatz means trouble," he said. He set his jaw with determination and called down the hall. "Swenson! Get us the train schedule.

"Let's get going, Mimi. Forget about suitcases."

Tilly left immediately after handing Max her business card. "Keep me informed," she said.

CHAPTER FOURTEEN

Consequences

Ignatz was exhausted from watching his two prisoners. It had been only a few hours, but it felt like days.

Several annoying bright alley lights shone through the high windows of the warehouse walls. He had tried to turn off one dim bulb, but had jerked the dirty string too hard, and it broke off. As it was just out of reach, he couldn't unscrew it. It didn't seem so dim now.

Closing his eyes, Ignatz tried to picture himself drinking lime Kool-Aid and eating Twinkies on a sandy beach in the Caribbean.

He had secured Katrinka in a far section of the warehouse. That expanse appeared to have been vacated earlier than the area where he now sat watching Morgan. Although it was inconvenient to walk the entire stretch between the two of them, there couldn't be a better setup. With no windows at eye level, there was little chance of their being discovered.

Ignatz yawned. "Just think about this," he said. "If you

want outa here, you gotta ask your old man for the cash."

Morgan shifted his weight and looked straight ahead, as if thinking.

"It's not my father's problem," said Morgan. "I won't negotiate under any circumstances."

Ignatz chewed his nails as an aid to comprehension. "Yeah, right," he thought. "We'll wait and see." He frowned and took a quick breath which sounded, quite by accident, like the snort of a small pig.

Ignatz made the best of it by looking as unpig-like as possible. He even spat on his hands and slicked back his hair with his usual dignity. "I could bust the nose on that two-timing dame," he muttered.

"You could do a lot of things," said Morgan, "but it doesn't make you free of the consequences."

"You think?" said Ignatz. Then he remembered. "Oh, yeah, I seen it on TV. That show, *Truth or Consequences*. Bob Barker passes out lots of consequences," he said, "but you're not assembled proper to dish them out like Bob Barker."

Morgan looked him directly in the eye. "I don't have to," he said. "They'll just happen to you anyway."

"Like how?"

"Well, here's the way it works. You know why my father doesn't have the money available?" said Morgan. "It was because of what you did to the animals. He gave his money for an elephant sanctuary. To protect them from people like you."

"No lie!" said Ignatz. He puffed out his chest with the pride of a newly recognized mover and shaker.

He had a new thought. "I can play Truth or Consequences too," he said. "When you two don't tell the truth, meaning never, then I get to make up a consequence."

Morgan straightened his back and jerked his head around to face Ignatz.

"You won't need to involve Katrinka," he said. "You

and I can work it out."

"Sorry, Mr. Morganthal. No can do."

"But Katrinka has nothing to do with it," said Morgan.

"Ha!" said Ignatz. It sounded so manly the way it echoed from the warehouse walls that he tried again, with even more impressive results.

"Ha!"

The sound of his own voice increased his courage.

He coughed his best social cough to announce a forthcoming statement. "I got something real preponderant to say." He crossed his arms to make his proclamation. "You two are getting married," he said.

There was no change in Morgan's expression.

"Me, I got it all set up," said Ignatz, "real legal and all. It's all in knowing the right people. I got connections, see. That'll shake out the money."

"You can't make a couple marry against their will," said Morgan.

"Really?" said Ignatz, picking his teeth. "Your two-timing dolly ain't exactly dragging her feet." He raised one eyebrow and slowly sucked the air in between his teeth.

"Maybe," said Morgan, "but there's no room for discussion. It takes two. What made you think I'd go along with it?"

Ignatz narrowed his eyes. "Henrietta Lawrence," he said, "that's what."

There was no response.

"You lied to me," said Ignatz. He tried to look directly at Morgan, but he had to avert his eyes. "Uh, to be entirely vivacious," he said, "I suppose it was Katrinka implicating it. Anyways," said Ignatz, "you should have told me about this Henrietta. So *she's* your main squeeze! You want to save her neck? You're getting hitched. But it's to that Katrinka."

The blood drained from Morgan's face. "I see," he said.

"What will it take?"

Now with Morgan ready to cooperate, Ignatz found it convenient to employ his mysterious look once again. It would buy him time to do some strategic planning.

He asks me what it'll take. Well, I would tell him, excepting I don't know. The big thing is, I gotta get them hitched, which they won't do unless I lock up this Henrietta.

I'll keep her till they're done getting married. Trouble is, I gotta find her first.

He thinks I got her already! Ha! Let him think it, 'cause I will, soon as I figure out how.

If I told him it was Katrinka set me up to do this.... Whooee! He'd have a cow! Trouble is, if he's mad at her I'll never get them hitched. I better keep mum, like as if she's a angel or something.

But this Morganthal guy, he's real cool. How's he pull it off? Bet it's 'cause his name ain't Beverley.

But you never can tell, maybe he's got a girly name, too. It could even be Lizzy-Lou, or something like that, and he wouldn't care.

If it really was his name, and some guy says to him, "What kind of a idiot has a name like Lizzy-Lou?" I betcha he wouldn't even pop 'em in the kisser.

I don't get how he seems like a regular guy anyways, but I still don't guess he'd pop 'em one.

I could stop caring too, but I'm used to how my name makes me mad. And being mad, that's who I am.

So how's he pull it off? Like when I keep forgetting about his food, and he just says he knows I got lots on my mind.

The thing about my job with the elephants and stuff, I gotta do like in the movies. You can't get all soft and wimpy, and thinking like they got feelings, or people won't think you're a real man. Leastways, when I'm out there with that whip, ain't nobody thinks I'm a Beverley.

Well…but I guess ain't nobody thinks Morganthal's a Lizzy-Lou, whether he does stuff like that or not.

Ignatz felt somewhat puzzled by the challenge of being a man. He kicked a chunk of cement into the corner. It shattered against the wall, next to the rattrap.

He remembered hearing that a trapped animal, if it was desperate enough to be free, might chew off its own leg. "That just proves it," he thought. "They don't have no feelings."

He glanced at Morgan. "Maybe he's got feelings," he thought. "I wonder."

But there's another way to think of him. He's the guy who found me out, right there in the ring. Pinned me down in the sawdust. It's nobody's business if I got barbs on my whip.

Just a week before that, I seen him in the spotlights. He was a clown, juggling balls on a unicycle, like his old man used to do. So, what all of a sudden made him into a big shot police type?

Except for him catching me, nobody had to know. And he says consequences happen anyways. Ha! If nobody knows, then what kind of consequences is there?

Unless it's how we interspect with ourself.

Ignatz wasn't through thinking it out, but he had business elsewhere. "Hey," he said, "I gotta split."

He hurried toward the far section of the warehouse. There he found Katrinka slumped forward in her chair. He told her it was high time she got ready.

Her eyes filled with tears. "How do you expect me to do that?" she said. "Wait till Morgan sees he's marrying a girl with dirty hands and no wedding dress! She sniffed and peered at him from the corner of her eye. "He has a real violent temper, you know." A large tear ran to the tip of

Katrinka's chin. "What kind of a monster are you?" she said.

Her lips were pale and colorless, but her eyes were pleading with him. Ignatz realized only twelve hours ago he was expecting to be her hero.

"Well," he said, "you can lie, and stuff like that, but me…I say you can't be free of the consequence."

For a moment, she stared at him as if she had heard that somewhere else.

"I want to get my wedding dress," she said quietly. "It's at the hotel. If you let me, I'll come back," she said. "I really will." Katrinka attempted a weak smile and blinked her eyes.

"Maybe you will and maybe you won't," he said. "But I ain't no fool."

Ignatz sincerely hoped Katrinka might concede that he wasn't. She said nothing.

Suddenly Ignatz brightened. "Know what?" he said. "I conjured how we can get Henrietta! Mr. Morganthal can make her come."

"He won't ask her to come," said Katrinka, "but *I* could get her here."

"You think?"

"Yes, yes…Hetty'll come!" The dimples appeared in Katrinka's cheeks. "And when she does, we can give her my key," she said. "The dress is in a box under the bed."

"Right. She'll take care of you real good. Like you deserve."

Right off, he would tell Hetty what Katrinka was up to. "I seen those roller derby gals tussle," he thought. "I know what Hetty'll do to that two-timing dolly. So what if she slaps Katrinka around? She's got it coming. Fair's fair."

Ignatz would show them all he was nobody's fool.

He imagined Katrinka in a wedding dress. "She'll be a real looker," he thought, "even with a black eye."

Ignatz figured his conscience would be clear. After all, there was nothing he'd done so far except pass around a few well-deserved consequences, like on the game show.

"The preacher guy's coming," he said. "I ain't got time to shoot the breeze."

Then to commemorate her special wedding day, Ignatz untied Katrinka's hands and gently secured both ankles to a vertical pipe instead.

Like Zorro

Ignatz called Hetty and told her Katrinka was in trouble. He explained where to come then he sat back and waited. He had a vague impression Hetty suspected he had set a trap, but Katrinka was right; Hetty came quickly.

When she arrived, Ignatz decided Hetty must be somebody special. "Not a snazzy dame like you'd whistle at," thought Ignatz. "Not like Katrinka. But seeing her, you want to check your deodorant ain't wore off. She's real straight and tall and she doesn't look scared."

He warned Hetty to follow his instructions. "It ain't just about Katrinka," he said. "You see, I got me one Morgan Morganthal, too. Here's the deal," said Ignatz, "You do like I say, and I don't kick his bucket."

Hetty picked up Katrinka's hotel room key and went to get the wedding dress as directed.

Meanwhile, Ignatz had some thinking to do while he waited for Hetty to return.

When she gets back, I gotta get myself real mad, like before. I better keep conjugating about how I been treated unfair. Elsewise, how's it supposed to work? I can't just say, "Hi, guys, just fork over the money and let's have a party."

I know.... This Hetty, she's sweet on Morganthal, so what I'll do is talk kinda through my teeth, like Jack Palance. "Now

listen up, see.... You don't cut out, and I don't cut his throat,"
or something like that.

I gotta think like I'm Marlon Brando so's they take me
serious. What good is a bunch of movies if I didn't learn anything?

Why are they getting me all mixed up? They're doing it so's
I can't remember about it being unfair, like at first.

Trouble is, how come she got me shaking hands with her like
she was a friend or something? I gotta think how she done that.

When I says to her, "What, you hate the name Henrietta, so
that's why they call you Hetty?" she says, "No, I like Henrietta
just fine. It was my birth mother's name."

When I says I got my mother's maiden name, man, that
was close! I pretty near let slip about my name being Beverley.
She says my mother must have been real proud to have gave me
her family name.

Ha! I says, I got me just one handle, and it's Ignatz.
Then she says, "You mean like Zorro or Tarzan?"

While he waited for Hetty to return with Katrinka's
dress, Ignatz decided to abandon the dramatic threats he
had rehearsed. He chose instead to strike his mysterious-
profile pose. So far, that pose had proven effective, and it
demanded less effort.

It came quite naturally for him to look heroic. "Yeah,
that's me. Like Zorro," thought Ignatz. "I like that." He now
stood a little taller.

Questions Without Answers

Hetty walked slowly to Katrinka's hotel room. It would
take time to think through the circumstances. She tried to
narrow her thoughts to the key questions.

Where is Morgan? Why is Ignatz holding him? Maybe he wants money.

Should I run to the police? No, maybe Ignatz would retaliate. He may be unstable or unpredictable.

What if Morgan is working out an escape plan, and I upset it? Things could get worse by my blundering into it before I know more.

But why is he holding Katrinka, while I'm free to walk around?

I think I know why. He can control me by threatening to harm Morgan. He could have called to say it was Morgan who needed my help. So why was it Katrinka he told me about?

He may not want me to know where Morgan is, or maybe Ignatz doesn't want Morgan to learn he has control over me. Or possibly Morgan doesn't want my help. Why? Because he wants to marry Katrinka?

If he does, then maybe their marriage will be legal like Ignatz says. Morgan tried deliberately not to look at me in the convention. It could be that he didn't want to face me and have to say he and Katrinka had made plans.

No. He would tell me. We've always spoken openly. So why did he disappear?

I haven't spoken with him for so long I can't be sure. The week they were planning Phil's funeral, did he see Katrinka in a different light?

Ignatz seemed to Hetty like a one-man wasp nest. As long as no one angered him, he probably posed no danger. Maybe the answer was to cooperate with him unless a better idea should arise.

Hetty thought of the beautiful silver wasp nest outside the cottage gate. The feeling of protection the porch provided was no mere illusion. Over time it had become the very haven Hetty only imagined it to be in earlier years. The wasps came to recognize their boundaries, or so it seemed.

It was comforting to imagine sitting on the stone steps in front of the cottage.

The graceful arch of ivy over the door; the roses climbing the trellis at the gate. When the gate opened into the carefully laid stones of the path, a friendly squeak of the hinges announced someone was coming.

Many feet followed along the low picket fence, disturbing the green softness in the crevasses, but the delicate mosses forgave trespassers and continued to spread underfoot. Hetty tried to picture every sweet detail.

There's so much love in the cottage, I can feel it from this far away. If I imagine I'm there, maybe it can protect me from whatever Ignatz has in mind.

How can I protect Morgan? And I have to think of Katrinka.

Without more information, I'm not sure yet how to answer my own questions.

I can't use weapons I don't have.

I need the strength to love Katrinka and trust Morgan. That's all I have.

Friends

When Hetty returned with the wedding dress, Ignatz drew his eyes into a confidential squint for her benefit.

"This Katrinka," he said, "she's got you all messed up, you and Morganthal. Looks like she's had dibs on your man all along. Now she's got her claws in him, for sure." Ignatz laughed. "That's one double-crossing dame," he said. "How did you make a enemy out of a humdinger like her?"

Receiving no answer, Ignatz flexed his best bicep and sniffed. "You oughtta give that dolly what she deserves," he

There's so much love in the cottage, I can feel it from this far away.

said, "if you know what I mean. No monkey business, and she stays tied up."

Hetty waited in silence until it seemed likely Ignatz had left, then she approached Katrinka from behind. "We'll do just as we're told," she said.

Katrinka stood with her ankles secured to the pole. She had been listening for footsteps and crying softly. "Hetty?" she whispered. "I was afraid you'd get lost." Her nose was running. "I'm sorry I got you into this, Hetty," she said, "but I needed you."

Hetty opened the box to reveal several towels and washcloths, both wet and dry, tucked in the corners. She had also brought Katrinka's bag of cosmetics.

"About the wedding dress...." said Katrinka.

"It's a little wrinkled," said Hetty.

"What I meant is just...well, I can explain why I brought it here."

"There's no need," said Hetty. "But we'll have to get you ready before Ignatz comes back."

Katrinka held onto the pole. "I'm not sure I have the strength," she said. Her voice was weak.

Hetty pulled the chair close to where Katrinka stood and then struggled to loosen the ropes around her ankles until they gave way.

When Katrinka was able to sit, she put her head in her hands, and her dirty fingers smudged her cheeks. "You'd better tie me up again real quick," she said. "I hate Ignatz."

"Yes. We mustn't anger him," said Hetty. She tied Katrinka's ankles to the legs of the chair and cleaned her cheeks with a damp washcloth.

Katrinka closed her eyes and leaned back against the pole. "I'm so tired," she said. Her voice broke, and she let her limp hands lie in her lap.

When Hetty had gently wiped around Katrinka's eyes,

she swabbed her face until it looked fresh. Holding each hand, Hetty tenderly wiped Katrinka's sticky fingers. She gave careful attention to the grime in her nails. It appeared she had painted them as recently as yesterday when she was back home at the gatehouse.

There was only the slightest tremor in Hetty's hands as she brushed Katrinka's hair. "I should have thought of the toothpaste," she said. She looked around as if realizing how worthless toothpaste would be without water.

When Katrinka was through using the toothbrush, Hetty held the facecloth to her mouth so she could spit in it. Taking the wedding gown and veil out of the box, Hetty hung them by their two satin hangers on a protrusion high on the cinderblock wall.

Katrinka was pale and still as she watched. "It wasn't supposed to happen like this," she said. "So sleazy."

"We won't *let* it be sleazy," said Hetty. "You're going to look too pretty for that."

"Can you do it, Hetty?" asked Katrinka. "I mean, can you put on my makeup? Before the dress, I think." Hetty leaned over the box and picked up a pink bag of cosmetics and looked inside.

"Sorry," said Katrinka. "I didn't mean I was afraid you'd miss my face or anything like that." She made a small smile.

"I know," said Hetty, "but there's not much light in here. And I know nothing about eyelashes like these."

"I won't need them," said Katrinka. "Morgan won't care about the eyelashes. He'll want me to look more like... more like you." Her eyes filled with tears.

Hetty walked behind Katrinka to hide her emotions. "Let's make it the best day possible," she said, placing her hands gently on Katrinka's shoulders. "You have to promise to love him," she said. "Tell me you'll see all the good in him. He'll do that for you."

Katrinka nodded.

"I know you love the way Morgan cares about people. And how he listens to what they say. Please say you do."

Katrinka sniffed and nodded again.

"It's how your father taught him," said Hetty. "The way he grew up," she said. "But you know that. When they were performing, nothing they did was just a gag. Morgan was learning to be careful with people's feelings the whole time. And it was Phil who explained the facts of life to him while they sat together sewing costumes."

Hetty's lip trembled, but her hands were steady. "I think you'll see your father in him every day."

Katrinka sighed and decided she should put on the dress immediately, with no regard for makeup. She was afraid Ignatz might arrive at any time.

The long train was double-hung over a second tier of the hanger. Hetty reached for it and held it high off the dusty concrete floor to protect the clusters of tiny seed pearls around the edges of the lace.

"Morgan doesn't pretend to be as good a clown as Max or Phil," said Hetty, "but he has sawdust in his veins."

"I know," said Katrinka. She looked at the floor. "It's no secret his father wasn't involved in his life, growing up," she said, "but that's changing, don't you think, Hetty?"

"Yes, I'm sure of it. And Max and Mimi must seem almost like parents to you. They've always cared about you."

"How can this have a happy ending?" said Katrinka. "I hate Ignatz."

Hetty carefully lowered the wedding gown over Katrinka's head. She bit on her lip. "Sometimes it helps me to remember everyone started out new," she said. "Like Ignatz. He used to be a small person with no mistakes in him, when he was born. Don't you guess what he needed was the same as everybody else? Maybe he's still trying to find it because things went terribly wrong for him."

"I bet anything he wanted to be a hero," said Katrinka, "like in the comic books and movies. But if you ask me, he's a villain."

"Well," said Hetty, "have you noticed how many villains started by trying to save the world or something marvelous and dramatic? They only sour on the idea when they feel misunderstood. Actually," she said, "if we all listened to each other like Morgan does, maybe there wouldn't be as many villains."

She paused. "I'm talking too much," she said.

"No. Honest, Hetty. It helps." Katrinka closed her eyes. "Are you my friend, Hetty?"

"Yes, we're friends.

"Do you think it will always be that way?"

"Yes, Katrinka," she said, "but here's how it will work...." Hetty fastened the last button at the back of the dress. She was unable to steady the trembling in her hands. "We'll be friends...."

She embraced Katrinka. "It's just that afterwards...you won't be seeing me.

"Not after you and Morgan are married."

CHAPTER FIFTEEN

The Holding Pen

Hetty could hear Ignatz lurking around the corner by the door. He seemed to be shuffling keys and other assorted objects until at last his footsteps faded for a time.

But it wasn't long before they heard him return. He coughed and spat in the corner, probably as a way of announcing his entry. Or maybe to signal the end of his eavesdropping, with no need of confessing to it.

At the sight of Katrinka, Ignatz froze in place. "Wooeee...." He said, "Oh, my! Ain't you a sore for sight eyes, I mean....You know."

When he gathered his wits, he garbled a few more words.

"But you can't fool me," he said, "like as if you was a angel. Anyways, how do I know as I can trust you? I don't get it, seeing as how you're friends and all." He glanced at Hetty and puzzled briefly.

Suddenly an answer came to him, and he said, "Hey! I know where I can put you till they're married."

The back alleys were poorly lit in most places, but Ignatz
seemed to know where he was going. Hetty was surprised
to learn he was keeping Morgan in the same warehouse as
Katrinka. If only she had felt his presence when they were
under the same roof!

Though Ignatz walked rapidly, Hetty kept up the pace.
She knew her careful cooperation was the key to Morgan's
safety; the only one she could control.

As they walked, they spoke few words. Hetty was grateful
for the silence so she could concentrate on landmarks along
the route. They might help her retrace her steps back to
Morgan. She noticed the elm trees arching overhead from
the left. Even the hum of electrical wires over the diagonal
walkway might help her find him.

Next to a dumpster, a can of orange soda lay on its side.
Its contents had leaked along a crack in the sidewalk to
form a streak pointing toward Morgan.

They passed a chain link fence with a sign that read
Beware of Dog. Someone had added a crooked "s" after the
last word. When two large mongrels leapt to attention and
snarled through the fence, Ignatz pulled Hetty away from
the streetlights, and they walked faster.

As they crossed the railroad track, their shoes scuffed
over the gravel between the ties. Hetty knew those tracks
led back to where Morgan was—where he would soon see
how beautiful Katrinka looked in her wedding gown.

"Step it up, Missy," said Ignatz. "I gotta meet the
preacher man before it gets light."

They followed the track about twenty more minutes
before Ignatz opened a heavy gate. "Ain't no point you
making a ruckus," he said. "Nobody around to hear it."

They walked across a hard packed dirt surface. There he
fumbled with a pair of handcuffs until he had fastened her

to a sturdy metal rail near the center of the clearing.

"This used to be a holding pen, back when I was with the circus," he said, "Like for switching animals around. Sometimes they kept them here a bit before they got sent, you know, wherever."

"What are you going to do with Morgan, Ignatz?" She waited, but he remained mysteriously silent. "I've been thinking, Ignatz. Maybe you could still let him go as soon as they're married. Even if they can't get you the money right away."

"What, you're saying like I gotta wait?" he moaned. "I had my plans configured all perfect. I mean what's the point in being rich, if you can't get your own money?" Ignatz laughed nervously. "Can't rich people figure out stuff like that?"

"Well," said Hetty, "if Morgan said he would, he'll do his best."

"In actual fact," said Ignatz, "it was that two-timing Katrinka. It was her what said Morganthal would get rich if he married her."

"She's right," said Hetty, "but you may want to get away before they hand you the money. Go before anyone gets hurt."

"Right!" he said. "Before there's consequences, like he says."

"And if you keep me here," said Hetty, "you know he'll send it."

Ignatz chewed on his lip. "I get it! Long as you're here, he gotta fork it over."

He dropped his keys and fumbled with picking them up.

"I think that would work, Ignatz."

"Hey now, Missy, I just thought of a problem. Maybe he won't need you anyways, once he marries that dolly."

"You may be right," she said, "but Morgan will want me safe. He'd feel that way about anyone."

"Ha! Anyone excepting me."

"He'd feel that way about you too, Ignatz," said Hetty.

"You think?" Ignatz was quiet for a moment. He seemed to consider Hetty's statement.

He sucked the air in through his teeth. "How am I supposed to kreep tack of all this stuff? Uh…I mean my plan was intrinsic enough already," he said. "I don't like it getting more harder than before. And now you say I oughta keep you here. You crazy?"

He rolled his eyes. "Man," he said, "that Katrinka! Ain't she a looker? Not that I noticed, or nothing. I don't guess Morganthal's complaining about that!"

Hetty looked at the ghostlike trees around the outside of the pen. The strange shapes shrouded in darkness did not frighten her as much as the uncertainty Morgan faced.

She could take whatever Ignatz was likely do with her. Perhaps it was because of her newfound strength. She had the power to control her feelings toward Katrinka. It hardly mattered to her whether or not she could count on that friendship. By expelling the ugliness of her emotions, feelings of peace promised to replace Hetty's recurring fears and nightmares.

Oddly, she also found comfort in the elephant odor that lingered around the pen. Hetty had become accustomed to it the summer she and Morgan cared for Blossom. The smell always clung to her hair and clothes long after she got home in the evenings.

Hetty closed her eyes and imagined she was with Morgan, working by his side. She remembered when they coiled the hose at the end of each workday, and sometimes their hands would touch.

Ignatz said, "You gotta be crazy."

Hetty knew this was no time for weakness. She dug her nails into her palms to hold back the tears.

"Maybe so," she said. "But keep Morgan safe."

The Nonsense Quotation

Ignatz slammed the heavy gate to the animal pen behind him and left for the wedding ceremony at the warehouse. According to him, both Katrinka and Morgan felt fine about getting married.

When Hetty found herself alone, her thoughts went to Morgan and Katrinka. She wondered what they might be saying.

Maybe he'll say, "Until I saw the way Hetty looked at the convention, I had never noticed an artificial side to her." He'll sigh with disappointment in me.

"I feel sure Hetty will go to law school," he'll say. "I'm sorry she's so dependent on me for inspiration. I'm worried she might flunk out. But I don't want to talk about her. Hetty and I were good friends, and I'm going to miss her terribly."

Katrinka will ask, "What do you mean by friends?"

Morgan will explain it this way: "A friend is someone who listens to you and shares your thoughts and ideas. Friends understand your feelings and want to know all about you."

Katrinka will ask, "So how might Hetty feel about you as a friend?"

Morgan will say, "All I know is when I'm with her, she can scarcely breathe. She becomes flushed when I look into her eyes. And if I sit with her at dinner and touch her hand, even by chance, she can hardly swallow. That's how she sees me as a friend."

Katrinka will say, "Oh, dear! I don't want to turn all pink and sweaty, drooling because I can't swallow and become unconscious from not breathing. It sounds miserable. And I wouldn't want to hear about your thoughts and ideas or have you learn all about me!"

Then she'll sigh sweetly and say, "Oh, please Morgan! Promise you and I won't have to be friends."

Morgan will generously comfort Katrinka with his heartfelt promise that they will never become friends. Then he'll say, "We must try to get on with our lives."

Katrinka will inspect her nails and say, "You mean our future of extravagant spending and delightful excesses, Morgan darling?"

He'll be puzzled and say something like, "Hmm.... Your sense of humor surprises me."

Then Katrinka will have a fabulous idea. She'll say, "I'm going to have Hannah made into a coffee table for your birthday!"

He'll say, "Hannah's not even dead yet! You're so quick with your thoughtfulness, Katrinka. It will be the perfect way to remember Hannah and Hetty. You do realize they'll need to be kept together, don't you?"

"Oh, yes," she'll say.

The hair will fall across his forehead, making him look more serious and thoughtful. He'll say, "You know they both have heart trouble."

Katrinka will be concerned. "You mean Hetty has heart rot, too?"

Morgan will explain, "No, she's not actually a tree, as it would appear."

He'll say, "Katrinka, are you sure you'll want Hetty in the center of the coffee table?"

"Of course, silly!" she'll say. "She would tip it over if we placed her on the edge, and that's where the magazines will go."

Hetty closed her eyes. A gust of wind lifted her hair to where it stuck to her mouth. Brushing her chin against her shoulder, she wiped it away. "Maybe I should think of something to be grateful for," she thought. "I know I could find Morgan. I'll always be able to find my way. I just need to care enough."

It took some effort, but she had another consoling thought. "I've done my part, even though things didn't turn out as I hoped. I set out to trust Morgan. I knew he would try to do the right thing. Isn't that trust? And to love Katrinka. Yes, I consider Katrinka my friend."

A small sense of wellbeing accompanied that realization.

"I cleared those two hurdles," she thought, "but what good has it done me? I'm handcuffed to a metal rail in a pen that smells of elephants. This is not exactly a high point in my life.

"I shouldn't be thinking like this when it doesn't cost a thing to be optimistic. Almost any nonsense would be better than feeling sorry for myself."

Hetty thought of the perfect foolish quotation for the moment. "*'Tis better to have loved and lost than never to have loved at all,*" she whispered. "If I could sit down with Alfred Lord Tennyson, I'd give him a piece of my mind…because it's not true…absolutely not true."

She bowed her head. "No, of course I agree with him. I shouldn't try to fool myself. What we had was too pure and good. How could those memories make me unhappy? When Morgan is gone, everything that was fine and right about him will always give me courage."

Hetty could see his face. The way his eyes crinkled at the corners when he smiled. And the smell of him. It was the fresh scent of sky when it's been washed clean by a spring rain.

She wanted to reach for him; to fly with him through the clouds, beyond the sky and higher, where everything is clean and bright…. Like eagles, lifting each other. Higher and higher toward the light. She closed her eyes.

"Hold my hand, Morgan. Don't let go...."
"Oh, don't let go!"

Dearly Beloved

Katrinka stood before Morgan, prepared for their marriage.
She straightened her shoulders and raised her chin.
"Dignity," she thought, "that's what matters now.

It's not the kind of wedding I wanted. So what! It's finally
happening, isn't it? Winner takes all. Hetty lost.
I can't help it if she thinks we're friends. She doesn't even
appreciate his money like I do. I was the one with staying power.
I can honestly tell Morgan Hetty didn't care enough.
That's it. Actually, she doesn't care at all. I'll tell him that's
why she helped me get dressed.
I'll tell him now, before the ceremony.

Even in the half-light, she could see the sadness in
Morgan's eyes.
The preacher held his head tilted rakishly to leeward.
Perhaps he feared the safety pins in his white collar were
inadequate to hold it in place.
"C'mon, holiness," whispered Ignatz. "Could you step
on it?"
"Hold your horses. I lost my place in this here Bible."
"Then find another place," said Ignatz. "Maybe that
part about still waters, or something?"
"Where's that?"
"How should I know? You're the preacher."
"I'll do it when I got the right place."
"Ain't it legal anyways?" asked Ignatz. "You promised
it's legal and all."

"Sure, long as I get my hundred clams," he said.

"Okay, okay!" said Ignatz. "Then just put your finger down somewhere, for crying out loud."

The preacher cleared his throat and began confidently. "Dearly beloved," he said. He opened the Bible cautiously, as if expecting a bolt of lightning. Squinting, he straightened his greasy glasses and bent close to the page. "It's too dark. I can't read it."

In an effort to salvage the ceremony, Ignatz peered over the preacher's shoulder at the verse upon which his finger had landed.

"It says here, *'The getting of treasures by a lying tongue is a vanity tossed to and fro of them that seek death.'"*

Death? Katrinka looked at the rattrap in the corner. There was something dead in it. Or was it just placed in her mind because of her lying tongue? Was that why she saw it?

It must be a warning!

For years Katrinka had hoped to carry a bouquet of miniature roses down the aisle. Pink roses with gardenias and baby's breath. As she looked down at her empty hands, her lips were firm. She fixed her eyes on Ignatz. Her hands trembled as if fearing what they were about to do.

Slowly she raised her arms, threw back her lace veil, and placed both hands at the back of her neck. "Here, Ignatz," she said. Inching up its gold chain, she removed the huge diamond ring from its hiding place deep in the bodice of her gown.

"Here's your money," she said. "Now give me Morgan's key. I want Morgan and Hetty's keys."

For four years Katrinka had treasured the sparkling diamond as the symbol of her dreams and ambitions.

The very instant it cleared her feminine anatomy, Ignatz hastened to claim ownership of it. In the palm of his hand, the magnificent gemstone dazzled Ignatz with a brilliance such as he had never seen.

He blinked stupidly. "Uh… keys?" He felt in his pockets. "I don't know about the keys."

"Then just go," she said. "Go and don't come back."

"Wait!" said Morgan. "Ignatz, where's Hetty?"

Ignatz hesitated then said, "North holding pen. I'll check on her, sir."

Packing as much holiness as possible into his peevish voice, the preacher-man whined to Ignatz, "It'll cost you fifty more, 'cause of the dim light. It's my policy."

Ignatz had other things to think about. Both men saw the advantage of disappearing and ran for the door.

Katrinka couldn't face Morgan directly. She said, "I've been awful."

"No, you've been clever and brave. I'm grateful," he said. "Very grateful.

"I say you deserve an Oscar for your acting. The way you went along with them," he said. "You convinced them we believed in their phony ceremony.

"There's no reason you should have been involved at all." Morgan tried to straighten his back, but the handcuffs didn't allow it. He shifted his weight and said, "I don't see Ignatz as a hardened criminal. He's more of a loose cannon, but a cannon can do plenty of damage."

Katrinka turned her face to the wall. "I'll find someone to cut you free," she said.

Morgan caught her attention before she hurried to leave. "You were generous and kind. Thank you, Trink." She knew he was pretending not to notice the tears on her cheeks.

Missing

When he found himself alone, Morgan looked around the floor of the warehouse. He noticed something on the floor where Ignatz had stood.

It was the keychain. If Katrinka brought the police with her, they could find Hetty right away. And now they had the keys to unlock her.

It was unfortunate Katrinka had left in such a hurry, but she was sure to come back and unlock his handcuffs right away. Meanwhile, he could do nothing but wait for her return.

While he waited, Morgan thought of Hetty's gentle voice and the sweetness of her smile, the soft blue eyes that revealed her unfailing trust and confidence.

He closed his eyes and pictured the graceful woman at the convention, the lights behind her forming a halo in her hair. That too had been Hetty.

Why did good things happen all around her? Even the love between his parents had been rekindled. How had she made it happen? Morgan smiled. Of course Ignatz would want to check on Hetty. It didn't surprise him at all that she inspired gallantry even in Ignatz.

A moment later, Morgan had a horrifying thought. Something Ignatz had said clicked in his mind. Didn't he say Hetty was in the north holding pen? And hadn't Max arranged for Blossom to be put there?

Like pieces of a puzzle, it all came together. Blossom had been transferred to that pen for observation. She would be considered dangerous and unpredictable until proven otherwise.

"No! No, not there!" cried Morgan. But no one heard him.

Hetty was in grave danger, especially if Ignatz were to check on her as he said he would. The elephant would never forget his cruelty. If Blossom were to sense his presence, it would send her into a frenzied rampage.

To help Hetty, Morgan would need to reach the pen before Ignatz. But first he had to free himself, and there was only one way to do it. He thrashed violently with a power he never knew he possessed, straining against the handcuffs that bound him solidly to the chair.

When the fire department arrived at the warehouse, a large crowd gathered to see the commotion. As one spectator remarked, "It's not every day you see a bride sitting in front between two firemen."

Katrinka led them to the place she had last seen Morgan. He was not there. They found only a twisted metal kitchen chair and a pool of blood on the floor beneath its bent and gnarled back.

Katrinka said, "Morgan didn't think Ignatz was dangerous." She asked the tallest fireman what to expect.

The man said, "He must have come back for Morgan." He used his radio to call the police. "Looks like we're too late, but maybe we can still save the girl."

CHAPTER SIXTEEN

Cautiously

Hetty wasn't sure how long she had been lost in thought. She was glad Ignatz had checked her handcuffs before he left to make sure they were not too uncomfortable.

In the early light, not much was clearly visible near her in the holding pen, but the grayish silhouettes of the trees outside the enclosure were becoming sharper.

Hetty thought of Hannah. It had always been a comfort to feel as if the magnificent oak tree understood her thoughts and feelings.

"Hello, trees," she said.

Something answered with a scuffling noise.

Hetty held her breath. There was no mistaking the sound. It was an elephant, and it lumbered toward her, getting closer and larger until she had to squeeze her eyes closed to make it stop being there.

The taste of fear was in her mouth as the elephant raised its powerful trunk.

In a moment of terror, Hetty felt the muscular tip of

its trunk on her neck. It was warm and a little moist. It wandered across her eyes, in her hair, and to her shoulders.

"Is it you, Blossom?" Hetty spoke quietly.

The elephant slowly caressed her cheeks, and the knob of its trunk was gentle as it stroked Hetty's face. Hetty wished her hands were free to return the greeting.

She and Morgan had cared for Blossom one summer, and the elephant remembered the bond they had formed.

"You do know me, don't you, girl?"

As Blossom's trunk came to rest by her nose, Hetty blew her breath softly into the opening, sharing with Blossom the affirmation of their friendship.

Hetty allowed Blossom to continue drawing in the air from her nostrils until the elephant ambled just a few feet away. Soon her immense form swayed happily from side to side.

In spite of the relief Hetty felt, she knew adult elephants were predictably unpredictable. The situation could become dangerous if the slightest breeze should lift her hair unexpectedly.

Hetty closed her eyes and remembered when Blossom had trampled Morgan. It happened because at that moment the elephant was reminded of the cruelty of Ignatz.

Morgan says elephants are a lot like people. Everyone has a breaking point, and that point is different for everyone.

Outside the warehouse, I noticed the string had broken off a bare light bulb. We had one like it in our basement, but Papa replaced a section of the pull-string with a rubber band. Ours never did break. That was because it worked best when we pulled with just the force it needed, but no more than necessary. The rubber band was a gentle way to avoid its breaking point.

With Ignatz, I didn't want to test his breaking point. When I saw that broken-off string, it made me look for more careful

Hetty felt the muscular tip of its trunk on her neck.

ways to tug at him.
The same goes for Blossom.

Blossom had a stick in her trunk, and she waved it like an orchestra conductor. Hetty tried to imagine she was sitting in the string section of the orchestra, holding her violin. But as Blossom came closer, Hetty felt uneasy.

Just then a quiet voice behind her said, "It looks like you're taking care of my girl."

It was a calming tone Hetty knew and loved. Did he mean Blossom? Why had Morgan come? She listened to his labored breathing and allowed an unfamiliar numbness to overtake her emotions.

The elephant stopped swaying.

Morgan's voice was soothing as he tried to release Hetty's handcuffs. "We won't let this disturb Blossom," he said. In the pre-dawn light, he worked as quickly as possible with the many keys on the chain.

Hetty saw a soft pink glow in the eastern sky. Katrinka's color. The sunrise must be happening for her. Hetty asked where she might be.

"Katrinka?" he said. "She's gone for help."

At last the handcuffs opened. "We'll need to move fast," he said. "Careful now. We should leave while Blossom is still happy with her stick. If Ignatz comes around, she could go berserk."

Once outside the pen, Hetty studied Morgan's face as he fastened the gate. At the sight of him, Hetty's breathing became rapid and shallow. She had to turn away and clutch the gatepost for support.

"I thought you'd be on your honeymoon," she said. It was a wooden, unnatural utterance, as if from someone else.

"I would be," said Morgan, "but you were tied up."

He turned to face her profile. Her cheeks were pale, and her fingers still gripped the gate.

Hetty's eyes were locked straight ahead in a blank stare. She tried to concentrate on Blossom.

"I need you to look at me," he said quietly.

A small moan rose from Hetty's throat. She was unable to face him. How could she hide the love he would see in her eyes?

"I hope you never for a minute thought it would be legal, Hetty."

"No, no," she said. "I mean.... I wasn't sure."

"Even if we *had* signed the marriage certificate," he said, "it would have been a meaningless piece of paper."

Hetty blinked with confusion. "But if it was what you wanted?" she said. "I mean, at the convention, when you left me...." she stammered, "I didn't know *what* you wanted."

"What I wanted! You make me crazy, Hetty, and you can't even see it? What I wanted...." Morgan's voice was strained with emotion, yet strangely lacking in energy.

Hetty now understood the cause of his emotions.

Her eyes widened and the color returned to her cheeks. She opened her mouth to speak, but upon turning to face him, she saw his hand and gasped. Now she knew why his voice had lost its strength.

"Morgan!" she cried, "What happened? You're bleeding! Your tie is drenched...." Her lip quivered. "You've lost a lot of blood."

"Oh, there may be some left," he said.

Before further explanations could be made, a yellow taxi drove up, and Max helped his wife to the curb. They had been followed silently by a fire engine.

Katrinka, in her wedding dress, sat nestled between two firemen. She allowed both of them to help her dismount and together they hurried toward Morgan.

Katrinka was the first to state the obvious. "Morgan," she said, "you're alive!"

"Oh, not entirely," he said.

Mimi wrapped Katrinka in her soft shawl and proclaimed they couldn't be more proud if she were their very own daughter, and they would forever consider her as such. Normally Katrinka loved being the center of attention, but when Max and Mimi thanked her for being Morgan's heroic rescuer, she squirmed with visible discomfort.

Morgan and Hetty had appeared so enthralled with each other that Max and Mimi put them together to wait in the taxi. Katrinka watched their heads in the rear window of the cab.

Morgan was content to have Max make all the decisions for him that day. But only as long as he could be with Hetty.

Goodbye

That afternoon, Katrinka held Mimi's shawl tightly around her shoulders and returned home to the gatehouse. She still wore her wedding gown.

Joseph was waiting for her on the doorstep.

He grinned. "Mr. and Mrs. Morganthal had high praise for you. They say you liberated everyone. But I see it hasn't gone to your head."

Katrinka sniffed and said, "Joseph, it was so humiliating!"

"If I know you, Trink," he said, "you could bounce back from anything. But I know it's awkward to accept credit when you don't deserve it."

He gave her a kindly smile.

"What you deserve is a good guy like me." Joseph's

laugh seemed to affirm the truth of his statement. "You're a high maintenance woman, Katrinka. There may not be a man on earth who could take care of you."

Katrinka appeared to listen with interest, so Joseph continued.

"In fact, you're so much trouble, I'd like to get started right away. When I showed you and your father around Australia, I left plenty to see for another trip.

"Come with me, Trink. We'll go right away. You're even wearing your wedding dress.... Just what the occasion demands."

Joseph laughed, but his expression was earnest. He waited for an answer.

Tears filled Katrinka's eyes. "He doesn't care about me anymore!" she cried. "I wish it was Morgan who loved me instead of you!"

Suddenly startled by her own words, her eyes widened.

Joseph held his breath as if hoping she meant to take them back, but she was silent.

"I've come to say goodbye, Katrinka," he said.

A Total Loss

Max advised Morgan to see a doctor about his wrist immediately; however, they waited until they were in home territory where Morgan could go to Dr. Davidson.

"So, I hear you were in a hurry to see your girl," said the doctor. Concern and friendly amusement showed on his broad face. He knew Hetty and Morgan well.

"Right, said Morgan. "She was kind of tied up."

Dr. Davidson left Morgan to wait in the examining room for a moment before preparing him for surgery. Although the muscle was detached, the doctor thought the nerve damage would be minimal. He invited Hetty to enter and wait with his patient.

Hetty was overjoyed at the first thing Morgan said. Mimi had told him she would not be satisfied until he and Hetty were married. They had been anxiously hoping for this response from his mother.

"Then there's nothing in our way!" said Hetty. "Unless it depends on what Dr. Davidson says."

"I suppose...." says Morgan. His skin was a pale grayish tone and glistened with cold sweat. "I suppose it does...."

"Yes, of course," said Hetty. His left hand was thoroughly bandaged, but she reached for his other hand.

"Morgan," she said, I have to know!" She closed her eyes and braced herself to hear the worst. Perhaps the doctor had prescribed a year of physical therapy in some hot mineral springs far away before Morgan could take on the responsibility of marriage. Maybe it would be a long recovery.

"Tell me, how long do we have to wait, Morgan? Exactly what *did* he say?"

In exchange for her fears, she saw joy and peace in his eyes. The serious deep blue of them offered reassurance. Morgan smiled, and his answer came in a whisper.

"He says my necktie is a total loss."

P. S. CHAPTER SEVENTEEN

A. Letter from Hetty to parents (excerpts):

To our Dear Parents,

Just this once, will the six of you forgive this group letter? We are so grateful for all the beautiful experiences you provided. If we were to thank you forever and ever, it still wouldn't be enough.... The sweet way you dressed Hannah—What a surprise that was!

Everyone can tell we're newlyweds. Wherever we go, we scatter rice —like Hansel and Gretel dropping breadcrumbs along the way.

Supposedly this ship serves wonderful food, but we're too seasick to try it.... Most of our time is spent leaning over our stainless steel wastebaskets. My husband (a beautiful word!) looks positively green. I love knowing he is really mine....

We are so indescribably happy!

Fondest love,
Hetty

We didn't mail this letter, so I'll add to it:

Now we're in the south of France.... We both fell asleep on the beach. Morgan is fine, but I got a bad burn. I'm totally untouchable. Morgan says I'm lucky my teeth didn't blister.

Morgan delayed his trip to bid on Ferris wheels in Germany until he dared leave me.... He flew all the way back here to see me for just half a day, instead of going straight to Czechoslovakia!

Those few hours with him were a dream come true. I'm so Happy!

All my love,
Hetty

P.S. We have the sweetest memory of little Danny planting acorns—the way he stood over them and waited for the baby Hannahs to grow. I know they will.

B. Letter from Max to Morgan:

Morgan:

My will and related trust documents previously provided that aspects of your inheritance were conditioned on your marrying Katrinka. I no longer see a need for those provisions. As of today's date, I have had them deleted from the documents. It has become obvious to all parties involved that your marriage to Hetty was based on a love of long standing, through numerous tests and challenges.

I was determined to make that fact absolutely clear, as my marriage to your mother suffered because she and others wondered if I chose her for her money. For that purpose I kept the condition in place even as you and Hetty were making plans.

At our invitation, Katrinka will continue to live in the gatehouse. Your mother and I appreciate your concurrence.

Respectfully,
Your father, Max

Enclosed are copies of the documents.

C. Letter from Ignatz to Morgan Morganthal:

To Mr. Morganthal,

I sure hope you got no hard feelings, because nobody else can help me.

Well anyways, this guy what lets me pick his mangos, he asked if I would go drown a sack of puppies for him, and I said sure why not. Before I done it, one of them pops out of the sack and licks my hand real devotional, 'cause she loves me right off.

I hid her in my shirt so people wouldn't think I'd went soft and mushy over a dumb animal. But then I says, who cares what they think, for crying out loud!

I named her Lucy and she ain't a bit dumb. We bought us a Whack-a-Mole business on the beach. She got real osteocratic taste in food, and she wags her tail real sweet and smart for the customers.

Anyways, Lucy got tore up pretty bad by a billy goat nobody had ate yet (of which there's scads here in Jamaica). Man, I wish somebody had ate that goat first, before it did that! I'd sure like to make it into jerky.

Now here's my question. The mango guy thinks my Lucy won't mend too good, so how can I make her more mendacious? If you got a idea how to elongate her life, it would at least be some constellation.

Your friend,
Beverley Ignatz

D. Letter from Joseph, sent from Australia:

My Dear Katrinka,

Thank you for your offer of marriage. I will give it careful thought. I confess I have never been entirely content to be merely your friend and confidant. However, I am a simple man and you are a complex woman.

If you are willing to work your way here to Australia on a freighter, I will consider your proposal a serious one.

My warmest wishes for your happiness,

Joseph

P.S. To answer your question:

No, I would not want to change you. It would be simpler to drain the ocean, and there's nothing you could say to change that impression.

E. Letter from Hetty to Katrinka:

Dear Katrinka,

Concerning your phone call earlier today, I do appreciate your confidence in me; however, I do not feel qualified to advise you in matters of the heart. I hope you didn't feel our conversation ended too abruptly.

It is enough to say you have truly found a prize in Joseph. Your father was wise to point you in that direction. Joseph has every quality you could hope for in a husband. The constancy he has demonstrated deserves your unwavering devotion in return.

I look forward to continued communications with you as your attorney and your friend.

Fondly,

Hetty

F. Thank you note from Hetty to Melinda Morganthal:

Dear Melinda,

Thank you for visiting us here in the hospital! Morgan and I are wild about the little elephant sweater, and when the baby can focus her eyes, she will love it too.

We were glad you approve of the name Philippa Maxine. As of today, we plan to call her Pippa.

We never expected this miracle to happen to us. I hope that excuses our rapturous descriptions of the way she blinks and grips our fingers, and even the way she breathes. You were amazingly tolerant to listen to us.

Morgan and I do not expect our behavior to improve.

We're so glad you can join us for blackberry cobbler at the cottage. Is a week from Wednesday at 7:00 still all right? I expect to be back on my feet by then. No family gathering would be complete without you!

Thank you for being the world's dearest sister-in-law.

Fondest Love,

Hetty

G. Reported in the Tilly Tells All gossip column:

Beauty queen Katrinka Wallace has been named Chief Executive Officer of Luvliness Conglomerates (LuvCon). Her fans will recognize the bold ad campaign she invented that catapulted her to this position: "Beauty is a gift you owe your loved ones."

Wallace maintains her husband, Joseph Ostler, is her inspiration and driving force. The conspicuously proud husband affectionately calls Katrinka "C.P." or "Centerpiece." The couple resides in the elegant gatehouse on the Morganthal estate.

Ostler will manage the growing elephant sanctuary for Max Morganthal.

Miss Wallace continues to be a popular guest on talk shows, where she explains her philosophy of beauty. Will we ever forget her confrontation with the stockholder who had developed a rash?

The angry woman demanded LuvCon resume the practice of testing beauty products on animals, "no matter how cute they look." Since that time Katrinka Wallace has seemed ill at ease unless accompanied by her attorney, Hetty Morganthal.

Which reminds me, dear readers: I received your many letters inquiring whether the gorgeous Morgan Morganthal and his wife Hetty had disappeared off the face of the earth.

I asked Max Morganthal personally. His answer was "Yes," but he said it with a smile.

Stay tuned!

H. Note from Morgan tucked in a book under Pippa's pillow:

My sweet Pippa,

You made my birthday a very happy one! Mommy says you helped her make the delicious cake. It takes a very grown up three-year-old to make blue stripes like that with a spoon. It seems like I just blinked my eyes and suddenly you turned into a big girl!

I hope you like the pictures in this songbook. Especially *The Bear Went Over the Mountain.* Shall we play *London Bridge is Falling Down,* when I get home from my business trip? I count five days.

Love,
Daddy

P. S. I love thinking of your mother whenever I look at you. Please give her a kiss for me and tell her I have more where those came from.

ABOUT THE AUTHOR

Award-winning author Martha Sears West grew up daydreaming and climbing trees in Bethesda, Maryland. Now the mother of three and grandmother of ten, West hopes everyone with children can see teenagers as the joy and inspiration she found hers to be.

West, who received her B.A. degree in linguistics from the University of Maryland, claims to have merely provided the hand that jotted down the story. She feels Hetty composed this book herself.

Hetty or Not is the third novel in the Hetty series by Martha Sears West. It follows *Hetty* and *Hetty Makes it Happen*. Her book titled *Rhymes and Doodles from a Wind-up Toy* is a collection intended for all ages. She has also written and illustrated two children's books: *Longer than Forevermore,* and *Jake, Dad and the Worm.* All Martha's previous books and audio books have received the Mom's Choice© Award for excellence in family-friendly content.

COLOPHON

The Bembo Typeface

Bembo is a classic typeface that displays the characteristics that identify Old Style, humanist designs. It was drawn by Aldus Manutius and first used in 1496 for a 60-page text about a journey to Mount Aetna by a young humanist poet, Pietro Bembo, later a cardinal and secretary to Pope Leo X.

More recently, Bembo is the typeface used for volumes in the Everyman's Library series. Monotype Bembo is generally regarded as one of the most handsome revivals of Manutius' 15th century roman type.

The font size of the italic sections in *Hetty or Not* is 13; otherwise, font size 12.5 has been used in the body of the text.

CPSIA information can be obtained at www.ICGtesting.com
Printed in the USA
LVOW08s0533010416

481626LV00007B/221/P